MW00937340

PALATINO FOR THE PAINTER

Thistlewood Star Mystery #2

C. RYSA WALKER

STARRY NIGHT BOOKS

Chapter One

ESTATE SALE

10–12 TODAY

EVERYTHING MUST GO!

THE HAND-LETTERED sign was barely visible between the cars parked in front of the modest brick house on Poplar Avenue. At least two dozen vehicles lined the curb, with several more in the driveway. Lucy McBride's home was only a few blocks from Main Street, so I suspected quite a few people had arrived on foot, as well. Small towns like Thistlewood don't get a lot of excitement, except in the summer when tourists flock to the area. It looked like half the town was taking advantage of this opportunity to snoop—and maybe pick up a bargain.

I'd printed a notice for the sale in last week's *Thistle-wood Star*, exactly as requested by McBride's son, even though I'd been tempted to tell him that no one around here would call the event an *estate sale*. Even when someone died, it was still just a *yard sale* or a *garage sale*, if you wanted to get fancy. Plenty of people would be snickering about how pretentious Kenneth McBride had gotten living off in California all these years.

On the other hand, given how far down we were having to park, it looked like he'd gotten an excellent turnout. Maybe he'd known what he was doing, after all.

Wren Lawson, my best friend, said, "You should take pictures of this crowd and post them in the classified section, with the caption *Classifieds Work*."

My daughter, Cassie, laughed from the backseat. "I'm not buying it. There are more cars here than you have subscribers."

I faked an offended look. "That's no longer true. I'll have you know we are officially in triple digits now. But to be fair, I suspect he pulled in at least as many people with the signs he was plastering downtown."

"True," Wren said as she craned her neck to inspect the cars parked along the right side of the narrow street. "I don't think all of these are locals."

She was right. Quite a few of the cars had out-of-state tags.

"Why would someone on vacation go to a garage sale?" Cassie seemed skeptical.

"Unless something has changed since the 1980s, Memorial Day weekend is kind of weird," I told her as I pulled into an empty spot two blocks down. "It's warm enough that people want to be outdoors, but the river is still wicked cold. So while the crowds aren't nearly as large as we'll get at the height of the summer, there's usually decent traffic at the shops. And this is just a few blocks from the shops, so..."

Wren nodded. "The diner was packed earlier. Guess some of them saw the sign and decided to check it out on their way down to the river."

As I got out of the car, my eyes drifted to the house on the opposite side of the street. Nostalgia hit me hard, and I could tell from Wren's expression that she was feeling the same. The house across the street, the one with the now-peeling blue shutters, had been like a second home to us when we were teens. I think we spent almost as much time there as we did at our own houses.

Tanya's place had two advantages. First and foremost was location. She lived walking distance from both the school and the diner. While very little that would interest your average teen tends to happen in Thistlewood, anything that *did* happen, happened downtown. The second advantage was parents who didn't hover. It's kind of hard to hover if you're rarely home. When we were at my house, Mom stuck her head in every half hour or so to check on us or offer snacks. Wren and her brother lived with their grandmother, and while Gran Lawson was a sweet lady who made really good oatmeal cookies, she didn't have cable or a VCR. As long as we didn't burn the house down or crank MTV up too loud, we had the basement to ourselves, so we were willing to deal with the fact that the food selection was generally limited to PB&J and microwave popcorn.

"I'd forgotten that Ms. McBride lived so close to the Blackburns," Wren said.

"Me, too. But I'm pretty sure the only time we were ever there was for the graduation cookout."

"True." Wren turned to look at Cassie, who was getting out of the Jeep. "Last time we were at Ms. McBride's house, your mom and I were only a few years younger than you. We were rocking eighties hair, pegged jeans, and shoulder pads, and we were ready to Wang Chung and walk like Egyptians all night long." She stuck one arm out in front and one behind her.

Cassie laughed. "I've seen a few of Mom's pictures from back then. What were you guys thinking?"

"Thinking we looked wicked cool," I told her. "And we were right. It's not our fault that your generation has no sense of style."

A flash of movement at the Blackburn house caught my eye. Did Tanya's parents still live there? Were they even still alive? A curtain on the upper floor flickered again, almost as if to say that at least someone there was indeed alive.

Or, far more likely, the curtain had simply moved because the air conditioner kicked on.

"Do her parents still live there?" I asked Wren. As the owner of Memory Grove, the town's funeral home, she was also an excellent source of information about which of our citizens had passed away over the past decade since she returned to Thistlewood.

"Her mom does," Wren said. "Her brother, too. Bud moved away for a while, but he came back a few years before I did."

"So, did her dad die?" I asked.

Wren shook her head. "Or at least, if he did, he didn't die in Thistlewood. He left town a few years back. No one even knew he was gone for the longest time. He and Bud never really socialized much. Pretty much the mirror opposite of Tanya and her mom."

Sally Blackburn had worked part-time when we were teens, managing the books at her husband's construction company. She'd kept busy the rest of the week with her clubs and church, so she was rarely home. And Tanya had definitely inherited her mother's social nature. If there was a crowd, you'd find Tanya in the middle.

The fact that Wren and I were her friends had been the only reason we'd made it through high school relatively unscathed. Like many small towns, Thistlewood tends to group people into two categories—*from-here* and *not*. Depending on the individual you're talking to, *from-here* might mean you've lived in town a few years, but more often it means that both sets of your grandparents were born in Woodward County, if not Thistlewood itself. My own family moved here when I was thirteen, and that fact, combined with my stubborn refusal to suffer fools gladly, meant that I was suspect. Wren and her brother came to live with her grandmother a year later, and their primary fault in the eyes of many Thistlewood residents was the color of their skin.

Our shared status as social outsiders in a teeny-tiny school had quickly forged a strong bond between me and Wren. In ninth grade, however, for reasons I've never fully understood, Tanya Blackburn—who was definitely *from-here*—thumbed her nose at her social circle by carrying her lunch tray over to sit with the two of us. The whole situation was touch and go for a bit, as to whether the others would accept us or shun Tanya. Her total indifference to the outcome was probably what decided the matter. She made it clear that the three of us were a package deal, and the center of gravity in the cafeteria gradually shifted to what had been the outcast table. There were still plenty of snide comments about me and Wren over the next few years, but Tanya pulled us into her circle through the sheer force of her will.

And then one day, the summer after graduation, Tanya was gone. Just up and vanished over the Fourth of July weekend. Packed her things into the back of her car and headed to Nashville, her parents said, without so much as a word of goodbye.

I hadn't believed it for a second. Neither had Wren. Yes, Tanya had been planning to move to Nashville, but she was going at the end of the summer. We were going to rent a place together. I was starting college in the fall at Vanderbilt. Tanya had no interest in higher education —she was going to find a job and try to land singing gigs at night. And as tough as it is to break through as a singer, none of us ever doubted that Tanya would make it. She would be the next Bonnie Tyler or Pat Benatar.

Wren, who had wanted to be a doctor back then, had joined the Army to earn cash for college. Once her enlistment was up, she would join us in Nashville.

We'd had it all planned out. In fact, we'd been planning it for two entire years. So nope. Wren and I didn't believe she'd simply run off. But, unfortunately, we were pretty much the only ones.

Two men were carrying a dresser over to their pickup truck when we reached the McBride house.

"Got this for thirty dollars!" the younger one said to Wren as he sidestepped the realtor's sign, which now sported a SOLD banner. "Can you believe it?"

"Looks like you drive a hard bargain," Wren told him.

The man on the other end of the load, who I thought might be the younger one's father, chuckled. "I gotta teach you to haggle, boy. You should've offered him twenty. Pretty sure he'd have taken it."

We dodged a few people clustered around the open garage door and stepped inside the house. Wren suggested that we check out the upstairs first, since the drawer had broken on her nightstand and she was in the market for a replacement. Two of the bedrooms, however, were already stripped clean, and the only nightstand left had a note taped to the top saying that it had been sold to the people who purchased the house.

"Well, poo," Wren said. "Guess we should have gotten here earlier."

We wandered around a bit more, then went back down to the living room.

Wren smiled and ran her finger along the spine of one of the many books that lined the shelves of the living room. "This part of the house is so *very* Ms. McBride."

She was right. All you had to do was look around and you knew instantly what our former English teacher had loved most. If she wasn't standing in front of the class teaching, Lucy McBride's nose had always been deep inside a book. I once caught her hiding out in her office during a pep rally, which teachers were expected to attend unless they had some other pressing task. In her case, the "pressing task" had been finishing John Irving's *The Cider House Rules*.

Given the sheer number of books in this room, and on the shelves upstairs, I had the sense that she hadn't parted with many of them when she reached that final page.

Ms. McBride's teaching influenced my eventual career almost as much as my after-school job at the *Thistlewood Star*. Jim Dealey taught me the mechanics of reporting and the specific skills needed to run a small-town newspaper, many of which still came in handy during the twenty-six years I worked at the much larger *Nashville News-Journal*. Lucy McBride was the one who kindled my love for the written word and who honed my writing skills to the point that I tested out of freshman comp in college. I was her prodigy—during my last two years of high school, she entered my work in writing contests and sent me scholarship information for creative writing programs. I'm pretty sure she expected me to write the great American novel someday, and she'd been deeply disappointed when I'd opted to write the news instead.

"The world needs more beauty," she'd told me the night our senior class—all thirty-seven of us—gathered here at her home for our pre-graduation cookout. "More poetry, more imagination. That's what makes life worth living. Why not write stories that lift people up? That make them happy? Do you really want to spend your entire career writing about tragedy and corruption?"

I'll admit that her words stung a bit. But I knew she was upset about my decision, almost as if it was a personal rejection. So I'd simply smiled and said, "The news is important, too. Someone has to write stories that explain the world we live in. And I'll do my best to sneak a little beauty into the mix."

We'd kept in touch at first, but the last time I'd spoken to Ms. McBride was at my own parents' funeral nearly a decade ago. I'd planned to look her up when I moved back to Thistlewood last fall, but it was one of those things I hadn't gotten around to doing during that first miserable month, as I went about the many tasks involved in ending a marriage of nearly thirty years. I'd also just purchased what was left of the *Star*, which had been shuttered since Mr. Dealey died five years earlier, and was trying to figure out what I'd need to do to get the paper up and running again. The answer to that question had been "a whole heck of a lot," unfortunately, which had left me very little time for social calls.

As fate would have it, Ms. McBride had passed away peacefully in her sleep by the time I got settled. I didn't even have the online version of the *Star* going at that point, so I hadn't been able to post an obituary for her. One of the odd quirks of my former boss at the *Star* was his belief that every person's last mention in his paper should be distinctive. Your obituary was your final bow, he'd always said, and it should stand out, rather than blending in with a notice for a community garage sale being held in the local park next Friday. So he'd given every person their own special font face—some bold, some italic, some serif, some sans. For example, the former high school football coach died right after I started working at the *Star*. Coach Bailey was an obnoxious little toad of a man who'd routinely yelled not just at his team, but at pretty much everyone. Mr. Dealey composed his obituary in Times New Roman, a perfectly ordinary and respectable font. But he'd used small-caps. It was a subtle enough joke that most people missed it, but those who got it had to admit that it was perfect.

I'd decided to keep that tradition going, and if I'd been up and running in time to publish Lucy McBride's obituary, I would have chosen a pretty font. Something flowing like Lucida Calligraphy or Edwardian Script. Her love of beauty was reflected in the house she'd shared with her son, Kenneth, until he grew up and moved to California a few years after I headed off to college. It was a colorful house—not in a garish way, but with walls of seafoam green and pale yellow instead of the ubiquitous beige most people adopt. When we first arrived, a cheerful abstract print rug had still covered much of the hardwood floor in the foyer, but a man was now rolling it up while his wife dug around in her purse for some cash. The news that they paid a mere ten dollars for the rug seemed to start a chain reaction, and people were coming up to Kenneth, pointing at various objects, and throwing sinfully low offers his way. I didn't see him refuse a single one. He just nodded, as if their offer of fifty dollars was perfectly fine for his late mother's nearly new leather sofa. Maybe he didn't need the money. It was entirely possible that he just wanted this all to be over so he could go back to the airport and catch the next plane home.

"I don't think Ms. McBride would like this," Wren said. "All these people milling about, touching her things. Sitting on her furniture. She was a very private person."

"I know. It's a necessary step, though, if you're going to sell the house."

"True," she admitted. "The only real alternative is hiding things away in storage, like I did when I sold Gran's place. I should haul all of that stuff out and have a sale of my own soon."

I'd donated most of my parents' personal items after their funeral, keeping just a few mementos. But I'd never had to deal with putting their house on the market, since Cassie and I—and occasionally her father—had always spent a few weeks here in the summer, taking advantage of the river and the nearby tourist attractions in Pigeon Forge, Gatlinburg, and Sevierville. And in retrospect, keeping their house had been a very good thing. When Joe had his mid-life revelation and decided he was no longer in the mood to be married to me, I'd been able to pile my clothes and a few other things into the Jeep and simply go. It was a relief not to worry about divvying up furniture, dishes, and so forth.

The only thing I'd really missed from my life in Nashville was my daughter, and recent events seemed to have solved that problem. Cassie had decided not to return to Nashville after our misadventure a few months ago, when Edith Morton's killer held us at gunpoint. I was glad to have Cassie home, but the decision worried me. She'd had a life in Nashville, and a job she enjoyed. Was she staying because she wanted to be here, or because that experience had scarred her. She *seemed* okay to me, but what was there in a tiny mountain town for a girl in her early twenties? How long would she enjoy weekend outings like this one, accompanying her mom and her mom's best friend to an estate sale? When I was her age, I would have been bored silly. There was no force on the planet that could have convinced a twenty-two-year-old Ruth Townsend to live in Thistlewood, Tennessee.

"Do you know where Cassie went?" I asked Wren.

"Still upstairs, I think." She leaned toward me and whispered, "Cross your fingers that she hasn't found another diary. I don't have a key to this place, so sneaking in to return it would be much harder."

"Remind me to check her purse before we leave," I said. Cassie's curiosity was a large reason we'd wound up in hot water a few months back, but it was also a major factor in me solving the case. Not something I'd want to risk again, however.

Wren glanced over at Kenneth McBride, standing at the edge of the room with a dazed expression on his face. Human interaction didn't seem to be his strongest suit. Or maybe he just didn't like crowds.

"Oh, Ruth," she whispered. "Why did we come here? This is actually sad."

"I know. Do you want to leave?"

"Yes. But first I'm going to buy some of these books. I'll give them a good home. The ones I don't have room for, I'll donate to the library. How much do you think I should offer?"

"I don't know. Maybe you should ask him?"

Wren squared her shoulders as if she were preparing for battle and walked across the living room. I hung back, trying to stay out of everyone's way, and watched as she tapped him lightly on the shoulder. Her lips were moving, but I couldn't hear what she was saying over the ambient noise—a baby crying somewhere, laughter upstairs.

Someone stepped up behind me. I turned, thinking it

was Cassie, but instead found Dean Jacobs smiling at me. As usual, he was looking very handsome, something that's hard to pull off in a mail carrier's uniform.

"Good morning, Ruth."

"Dean! It's so good to see you. What brings you here?"

He looked around doubtfully. "I'm kind of wondering that myself. Not like I need anything else cluttering up my house. I should have a sale of my own, actually."

"You should team up with Wren," I said and looked down at my watch. "It's early. Mail already delivered?"

Dean laughed but looked a little guilty. "Nah. Just taking a quick break. Saw the sign when I was coming down the sidewalk and noticed your Jeep out by the curb." He glanced down at the floor. "I was sorry to hear about what happened to you and Cassie. Can't say I ever really liked the two of them, but I didn't think they were murderers."

"Greed can be a powerful motivator," I said. "I'm just glad that it's over."

"Yeah. Me, too. Is...um...Cassie staying in town for a while?"

I nodded. "Yeah. I think she's at sort of a crossroads. Trying to figure out what she wants to do next."

"Oh. Is she...here?" His face was turning red, and I laughed. I couldn't help it.

"You should come up and see us one night," I told him. "If not for you mentioning that Edith's door was locked the day she died, I might not have figured things out. The least I can do is cook you dinner."

He looked surprised. "Really?"

"Sure. Why not?"

"Do you think Cassie would like that?"

"I don't know," I answered truthfully. "I would, though."

"Then I'd love to. Just let me know when."

Cassie chose that moment to appear, and Dean flushed again.

"Good morning, Cassie."

"Oh, hey, Dean," she said, and then turned toward me. I wanted to laugh because she was so completely oblivious to the torture she was inflicting on the poor boy.

"I was just telling Dean he should come over for dinner sometime. What do you think?"

"That's a great idea. It's almost always just me and Mom. Sometimes Ed or Wren. I love them dearly but...it would be sooo nice to have someone closer to my own age around for a change." She turned her attention back to me. "Mom, I have to show you something. Hurry."

"Okay."

Cassie bounded off toward the kitchen and through a door that led to a garage. Dean and I followed. Lucy McBride's car had already been sold, and the smooth concrete floor was spotless. Plastic totes were stacked neatly in one corner, most labeled in the large, loopy handwriting I remembered from the blackboard as we discussed *Beowulf* and *Hamlet*. Decorations, apparently

—*Halloween, Christmas, July 4th*. I felt a little pang of sadness that these would probably never see the light of day again. No one was going to buy someone else's memories like that. I wondered if Kenneth would throw them out or pack them up to take back to California.

The one thing that seemed out of place in the almost obsessively tidy garage was a large cardboard box propped up against the wall next to the garage door. It looked like the kind of container that a mirror might come in—tall and wide but not very deep. Scrawled across the front in blocky letters was *Ruth Townsend— Thistlewood Star*.

"What on earth?" I said.

"Looks like she left something for you," Cassie said. "Come see. I have to confess that I already peeked."

I shook my head, laughing. "Now, why doesn't that surprise me?"

She pulled open the flap covering the end of the box. I reached in slowly to touch the frames stacked upright inside the package.

"Canvases?"

"They're paintings, Mom. Pretty good, too, based on the ones I saw."

She reached in and gently pulled the first one out.

It wasn't simply good. It was breathtaking. A large, vibrant tree took up most of the canvas. Some kind of weeping willow, maybe, but the colors were surreal. The trunk and branches were fairly normal, painted in a muddy, weathered brown acrylic. The leaves, however, were various shades of teal—some neon bright, some dark, and others almost transparent with the blue-green revealing the ugly brown below. *I'm here,* the brown seemed to say. *No matter how pretty the surface, I'm always here underneath.*

"It's beautiful," Dean said from behind my shoulder. "A little eerie, though."

I nodded. He had summed it up perfectly.

The world needs more beauty. That's what makes life worth living. Maybe this was her way of reminding me about that conversation so many years ago.

"They're *all* beautiful," Cassie said. "But why are they out here in the garage—and with your name on the box? Do you think she wanted you to have them?"

"I don't know," I said as I slid Lucy's painting back into the box. "Maybe I should go ask Kenneth."

"They'd look perfect in your office at the *Star,*" Cassie said. "The place needs some color."

She was right about that. I'd been thinking for months that the office looked kind of dreary. And now that I'd taken over the newspaper, it somehow seemed right to have Lucy McBride's artwork hanging in Mr. Dealey's old office to represent the two people—well, aside from my parents—who did the most to set me on my path as a journalist.

"I think that's a good idea," I told Cassie as I rummaged in my purse to see if I'd brought my check-book. I had a little cash on me but not much, since I really hadn't expected to buy anything. For the most part, I'd come because Wren mentioned it, and I thought it would be a good opportunity to get Cassie out of the house. And looking at her just then, showing Dean the other paintings, I thought maybe that was a very good idea.

I turned to see Wren coming down the steps into the garage. "There you are! I was beginning to think y'all left me here."

"Nope. Did you get the book situation worked out?"

Wren nodded. "Twenty dollars. I feel like I'm stealing them."

"If any of those are first editions, you sort of are. And knowing Ms. McBride, that wouldn't surprise me at all."

"I know, and I tried to tell Kenneth that, but he said he's just glad to know they'll have a good home. He's out of boxes, though, so I'm going to come back later, after all of this traffic clears, and load them into the trunk. If y'all are ready to go, I'm starved. Maybe lunch at the diner? And Dean, you're more than welcome to join us."

"Wish I could," he said, "but break's over. I need to get back on my route."

"Wren, come here," Cassie said. "Ms. McBride was quite the artist. And look." She tapped my name on the box.

"I'm going back inside to talk to Kenneth," I told her. "See what he'll let them go for. My office needs a little color."

"Huh," Wren said. Her voice sounded a little strained. "I didn't know she painted. He'll probably give them to you for free, though. I had to practically shove my twenty into his hand. And if she put your name on them..."

That was true, but I wondered whether the paintings were really something her son was willing to let go. These were things his mom created with her own hands. Originals. I was pretty sure that a piece of her soul had gone into these, and that thought caused my eyes to water.

Just then, my new iPhone—a late birthday gift to myself, and unlike my old one, capable of keeping a charge for more than an hour—chirped to life in my front pocket. It was Ed Shelton, who I guess I can call my boyfriend now, although that term sounds ridiculous for a sixty-year-old man. I motioned for the others to give me a second and stepped off to the side.

"Hey, Ed. What's up?"

I listened quietly for a moment and then told him I'd be right there. Even though the garage was stifling, I shivered.

"Mom?" Cassie said. "What's wrong?"

"Lunch will have to wait. That was Ed. Someone just found a car in the river. And there's a body inside."

☆ Chapter Two ☆

SMALL TOWNS ARE STRANGE PLACES, especially when it comes to death. When you live in a larger town and you read in the paper or hear on the news or even through the grapevine that a body has been found, you might idly wonder who it is. You don't, however, immediately assume that it's someone you know. In a town as small as Thistlewood, however, the odds are pretty high that you did know the person. There's an off chance that it could be a tourist, which would be awful in its own right, but your heart can't help but shift into overdrive at the news.

That's what I'd felt when Ed told me, and I knew that he was feeling the same. The odds that he'd known the person inside that car were even higher. Ed Shelton had served as sheriff of Woodward County for well over a decade. You don't win reelection three times without shaking a whole lot of hands.

I set off for the river with Wren riding shotgun. We hadn't exactly discussed her tagging along. It just sort of happened. Wren has this cool and calming way about her that I wouldn't trade for anything. It's what makes her so good at her job, and it also makes her an excellent person to have at your side during a crisis.

Cassie had opted to stay behind. She wanted no part in venturing down to the river with me when there was a body involved. I'd left her with my checkbook so she could negotiate with Kenneth McBride about the paintings we'd found in the garage.

"According to Ed, the car was spotted just this side of Jolly's Marina," I told Wren. "We need to keep an eye out for a fishing trail on the left. Should be the second one after the bridge, just past a large rock."

Okay, that's one other thing that I kind of missed about Nashville. Roads have names there, and they actually show up on the GPS. Here, except for major roads and those within the city limits, you were pretty much on your own, and instructions in Thistlewood were often maddening. First left past the big red barn. Then take the second right after Joe Wheeler's house. If you land in the river, you've gone too far.

That didn't seem very amusing now, with a car in the river.

Traffic was nowhere near the peak that we'd hit during the summer, but it was Saturday, so there were a number of cars headed to the river, loaded down with coolers and inner tubes. Most were semi-local, from neighboring cities and towns, just out for the afternoon. They had no idea yet that the river would be pretty much shut down for two miles or so downstream from the spot where the car was found.

"Do they have any idea how long the car has been there?" Wren asked.

"No. I don't think he knew yet. He told me they were just about to pull the vehicle out." There was a little nervous quaver to her voice that made me think the question was more than idle curiosity, so I added, "Why do you ask?"

"It's just that I hate processing drowning victims," Wren said. "Not much I can do with a body that's been submerged for any length of time."

"What are the effects on the body?" I asked, kind of dreading her answer but still wanting to know.

"Depends on how long the body has been in the water." She went on to paint a fairly vivid picture, which was more detailed than I'd have anticipated.

"You've had to deal with more than a few, I guess?"

She shrugged. "When you live near a river, accidents happen."

I turned onto the road Ed had mentioned, taking the ruts and bumps as carefully as I could. It wasn't much of a road, really. More of a wide path of beaten grass and dried mud beneath the tires.

"Thanks for coming with me," I said to Wren as we bumped along toward the river. "You're a good friend."

She laughed. "Hey, I broke into a house with you.

Compared to that, this is nothing. And I didn't have anything else on tap for today."

We passed a large metal sign riddled with bullet holes. *No Trespassing.* Judging from the tire tracks in the mud and the empty beer cans sticking up from the grass like bright metallic Easter eggs, it seemed that few people heeded the warning. I slowed down and maneuvered a particularly deep puddle, and as we rounded the small curve just beyond, the trees broke away, giving us our first clear view of the river.

The police had set up an amateur-looking barricade —yellow caution tape stretched between a dirty sawhorse and a tree at the edge of the woods. Two Woodward County police cruisers were parked on the left side, one marked *Sheriff.*

"Oh, look," I said. "It's our very favorite person." Even though I'd known Steve Blevins would be there, I felt a twang of disappointment. Any day that I could completely and totally avoid that man was a good day in my book.

I cheered up, however, when I caught sight of Ed leaning against the hood of his truck.

Wren grinned at me. "I see you looking out the corner of your eye at Ed, all cool over there by his Silverado. Can't say I ever imagined you falling for the cowboy type, but at least you picked a good one."

"Cowboy type? Ed?"

"All he needs is a hat and boots."

She did kind of have a point now that I thought

about it. I opened the back door and began digging around in the junk on the floorboard, looking for the zoom lens for my camera. I was glad I'd left the camera and various paraphernalia in the Jeep, even though it's a ragtop and Ed swears that one day someone is going to rob me blind. He's probably right, and when the tourists pour into Thistlewood over the summer, I'll need to be more careful. But some mornings, I'd forget my head if it wasn't firmly tacked onto my shoulders, so leaving the camera in the Jeep was the only way I could be sure I'd have it when I needed it. And yes, I could use my phone camera in a pinch, but I never really feel like I'm on the job unless I'm carrying my Nikon.

Wren gave the river a wary look. "I've got a bad feeling about this. Which is stupid. I see bodies all the time."

It was a little unnerving to see Wren rattled, especially when I was feeling nervous, too. I think it was partly due to Wren's description of drowning victims. We really didn't have any idea what we were going to find.

"Makes sense," I said as I pulled the camera strap over my head. "You're just used to them bringing the bodies to you. The accident or crime scene has a different vibe. You can wait here if you want..."

"No. I'm fine."

Ed smiled as we approached. "Well, you made it here in record time."

I nodded. "Camera was in the backseat, against the

advice of this ex-sheriff I know. So I didn't have to go back to the office."

"Right." He waved at Wren. "Brought your partner in crime, I see."

"Never leaves home without me," Wren said. "How's it going?"

"They're just about to bring the car up." He nodded toward Blevins and his deputy, who were standing at the river's edge talking to the tow truck driver. The truck was backed right up to the bank, and the thick chain snaked from the rear of the truck, disappearing into the water.

Blevins hadn't seen me yet, which was good. I raised my camera and took a few shots. The motion caught the eye of the deputy, Billy Thorpe, and he gave me a little smile, which I might have missed if I hadn't had the zoom on. Thorpe had been one of Ed's deputies back when he was the sheriff, and like most of the department, he preferred the old boss to Blevins. Ed had been forced to retire after he was the victim of a hit-and-run driver—a driver who was quite possibly Blevins's then-teenaged son—seven years ago during a routine traffic stop on New Year's Eve. The accident shattered his hip and left him with a decisive limp. He writes mysteries now. Good ones, too. Billy would probably lose his job if the man ever found out how much he shares with Ed. I get the sense that Billy might be the one who does the actual police work—the non-political side of the job that Blevins doesn't enjoy—so maybe that's his job security.

"Who found the car?" I asked Ed.

"Two brothers. Tourist kids, down from Ohio for a family reunion. They were trying out some new diving equipment they got for Christmas when they came across the car. At first they didn't know what they were looking at. It was partially buried in mud and silt. I can get their names from Billy later."

"So the car has been there a while?" Wren asked.

Ed nodded. "I would say so. They saw the body in the driver's seat when they went in for a closer look. Nothing left but a skeleton. Still strapped in the seat belt."

I shivered. It *had* been there a long time, then.

"Townsend!" Blevins bellowed from the riverbank.

"Oh no," I whispered in mock horror. "We've been discovered."

Blevins stopped at the sawhorse barrier. His face was red and he was already out of breath. "You need to get your girlfriend out of here, Ed. We don't need her or her camera making a bad situation worse. And Wren, we really don't expect you to pick up the body. If the family, whoever it might be, decides they need your services, we'll let you know."

Wren gave him a tight smile. The words were benign enough on their face, but we went to school with this guy. Blevins had never liked Wren, even told me that I was making a mistake by hanging out with *someone like her*. And there are certainly people in Thistlewood who've opted to take their recently deceased elsewhere rather than patronize a black-owned funeral home.

I wanted to punch the smug look off the sweaty face that Blevins was wiping with his sleeve. "Start of the tourist season," he muttered, "and something like this has to happen."

Ed's jaw was clenched. "Awful inconsiderate of the driver of that car. Sounds like he planned it all out. Drove smack into the river umpteen years ago just so he could ruin your Memorial Day weekend."

"I had to laugh at your lame jokes when you were my boss," he said, "but not anymore. And you need to clear out, too, Ed. You're a civilian now."

"Not by choice. And I know this phrase is overused, but it's a free country, Blevins. We made plans to meet here for a picnic this afternoon, and lo and behold, we find your fancy barricade blocking our access to the river. As far as Ruth goes, I don't tell her what to do, but her readers have a right to be informed. There's this little thing you may have heard of called the First Amendment?"

Blevins glared at him for several seconds, then jabbed a finger in my direction. "No pictures of the body."

"Are we going to do this same song-and-dance routine at every crime scene, Steve? I didn't take pictures of Edith Morton because it would have been ghoulish. That goes double for a skeleton."

Blevins rounded on Ed. "You told her that? How did you even know?"

"Come on, Steve. You weren't exactly using your

indoor voice when you were questioning those two kids. I may be older than you, but my hearing is still sharp as a tack, because unlike the guy who now holds my job, I was smart enough to protect my ears during target practice."

The sheriff ignored him, leaning forward across the barrier. It was definitely his indoor voice this time, because I had to strain to hear his next words. "I don't have to tell you how important tourist season is, Townsend. You actually have a few readers outside of Thistlewood after your little exposé on the whole Edith Morton drama."

He was right on that count. In searching for who killed Edith, I had inadvertently uncovered a much older murder. One of the TV stations in Knoxville had even sent a reporter down to cover the story a few days after I published it.

"So you need to tread carefully. Because if you scare off our business this summer, I can promise you that the whole town will be at your throat." Then he turned away and marched back down to the river.

"Such a pleasant man," Wren said.

"Indeed," Ed said. "He's just a big bundle of sunshine, lollipops, and rainbows."

"Are the divers still around?" I asked. "The ones that found the car?"

He pointed off to his right. "Jolly's Campground up the river. Blevins didn't close it. Although I'm guessing he did tell them to shut down river access."

"You said it was two kids, earlier. Did you mean *kids* kids, or older?"

"Older. Probably around Kate's age." Kate was his niece, who was a senior in high school. "Although, to be fair, I'm apt to call anyone under thirty a kid these days."

"Did these *kids*"—I made air quotes around the word —"already give their statement?"

"Yeah. They left just before you got here. Hiked back up to the main road. Kinda surprised you didn't see them on your way in."

"They must have cut through the woods. I didn't see anyone."

"Yeah, this area is pretty remote," he said. "The road is in bad shape, and since they expanded the marina, most people go up there. But we used to come out here to swim when I was a kid, and for...um...*private* parties when I was a little older."

"Did you, now?" I asked, giving him a grin. "Anything you want to share?"

"Nope. The main attraction was that it was a little less crowded on Saturday nights than that spot over there." He pointed upward at a spot above the tow truck.

I squinted my eyes against the bright sun. On the opposite side of the river, about seventy feet up, was a cliff, completely bare of trees.

"Lover's Leap," Wren said.

"Oh, yeah," I said. "I remember that place."

"Do you, now?" Ed asked, returning my earlier grin. "Anything you want to share?"

"Not in a million years. Do you think the car went off from up there?"

Ed frowned. "You know, I hadn't even thought of that. But it very well could have. There's a steel barrier up there now. We put it in when I was sheriff. Nothing especially sturdy—it's hard to get much into the rock up there without special equipment—but it was still better than the stupid rope they had strung across the edge before that. That rope was barely even enough to remind people where the edge was. But this car has clearly been down there a while, so..." He tilted his head to the side, and I got the sense that he was doing some sort of complicated geometry, trying to calculate where the car might have wound up if it originated from that cliff.

A grinding noise pulled our attention back to the tow truck as the chain was yanked taut and began reeling in its catch. River water dripped from the thick links, and the motor groaned in protest.

I watched the scene from my camera's viewfinder, snapping pictures in rapid succession. The front of the car rose from the dark water. It was covered in rust and mud, making it almost impossible to tell the original color. The only thing I could really tell was that it was a sedan. An old one. It looked like the headlights were knocked out because you couldn't even see a reflection. I was actually surprised there wasn't more damage to the front, given how hard the vehicle must have hit the water.

At first I thought it must be an out-of-state car,

because there was a tag on the front, and Tennessee only requires it on the back of the car. As I zoomed in closer, though, I noticed two things. The first was that the headlights weren't missing. They were just a relic of really bad seventies design on some luxury cars, where a metal eyelid closed over the light.

Second, what I'd thought was an out-of-state tag was a novelty tag. It looked like a normal Tennessee plate, but directly below the header were the words *B TYLER*.

The camera fell from my hands. It bounced against my chest instead of crash-landing on the ground, thanks to the strap. The day felt suddenly cold, like it was midwinter instead of late May.

"Ruth?" Ed said. "Honey? What's wrong?"

Wren's voice was calling my name, but it was like they were both inside a tunnel.

As the car rose from the water, I couldn't take my eyes off the novelty plate. Wren and I had crouched down next to the proud new owner of that rickety old Mercury Marquis Brougham thirty-three years ago as she attached that tag to the bumper.

"Oh my God, Wren," I said quietly. "It's Tanya's car."

☆ Chapter Three ☆

MY HANDS SHOOK ALL the way back to town. Wren had asked if I wanted her to drive, but I'd told her I was fine, mostly because she didn't look like she was in any better shape than I was.

B TYLER. How many times had the three of us driven around town in that old Mercury belting out "Total Eclipse of the Heart" at the top of our lungs? Tanya had always taken lead, since she had the same raspy quality to her voice as Bonnie Tyler. Wren handled the background vocals, and I did whatever I could to harmonize with them. I never was much of a vocalist, but any good karaoke singer worth his or her salt will tell you it's all about the spirit. And all three of us had spirit.

Everyone knew Tanya had big dreams. They'd heard her sing at talent shows and listened to her belt out the national anthem at the high school football games since she was in elementary school. So the rumor that she'd skipped town and headed for the brighter lights of the big city, it took hold quickly. It was the talk of the town for about a week, with everyone predicting that Tanya Blackburn would come strolling into town one day with a record deal and her voice blasting out of the radio. Wren and I, however, were telling anyone who would listen that it wasn't true. What made me truly crazy was that we couldn't even get Tanya's parents to believe us. They'd always seemed kind of distant, too wrapped up in their own lives to worry much about Tanya and her brother, Bud. And yes, Tanya was eighteen. But if Cassie had gone missing at that age, I'd have raised heaven and earth to find her, to make sure she was safe.

Wren had been dealing with her own family emergency at the time. Her younger brother, James, had an accident on his way home from a temporary job at one of the touristy restaurants. So I'd been the one who had taken the lead in trying to find Tanya. I called her house over and over, but nobody answered. Rang the doorbell, too. Nobody answered that, either, even though I could tell they were home. I checked with Pat and Teresa Grimes, who ran Pat's Diner before their daughter Patsy took over, and they said that Tanya hadn't shown up for work. Hadn't even called in.

After several days of this, I'd staked out the Black-burn house for a few minutes before the local women's club biweekly meeting. Mrs. Blackburn was president, and Tanya had said her mom had never missed a meeting. Around the time I figured she'd be heading out, I'd marched up the sidewalk and rang the doorbell. Then I knocked. Then back to the doorbell. Knock, doorbell, repeat. When Mrs. Blackburn finally answered, I'd been so stunned that I just stammered out the question, "Is Tanya sick?"

"I wouldn't know," Sally Blackburn had said, "because Tanya ran off. Packed her clothes and left without a word. Reckon she headed to Nashville like she was always saying she would. If she didn't tell you, it's because she didn't want you to know."

When I'd told her that this wasn't the plan, that Tanya and I were going to Nashville *together* at the end of the summer, Sally Blackburn had stepped out of the doorway and waved me inside. "You know where her room is," she'd said with a sigh. "Check if you don't believe me."

And so I did. Tanya's closet was empty. So was her dresser. The pictures on the mirror were still there, however. Not just the ones of the three of us, or of Tanya in her cheering outfit. If what her mom said was true, she might have left those. But she wouldn't have left the picture of her winning the talent show. And she wouldn't have left the notebook I saw peeking out from under the bed, the one where I knew she kept all of the songs she'd written.

Her younger brother, Bud, was in the hallway as I left Tanya's room that day. Tanya had always teased me, saying he had a crush on me. I suspected it was true. But he was nearly two years younger and still seemed like a kid to me.

"I don't believe it," I told him. "Do you?"

He shrugged helplessly. "She's gone, Ruth. I don't think she's coming back."

Wren had tried later in the week, asking if they'd heard anything yet, and she'd gotten the same answer. When I stopped in again a few weeks later, days before I was heading off to Nashville myself, Mrs. Blackburn hadn't been as nice.

"Tanya left us, Ruth. She left *you*. Maybe she just figured out she didn't want you hanging around anymore but didn't know how to tell you without being mean about it. So just drop it, okay?"

Those were the last words Tanya's mother ever said to me. I never went back after that. Neither did Wren.

"*B TYLER*," I said out loud. "I can't believe..."

"Pull over," Wren said from the passenger seat. "I think I'm going to be sick."

The Jeep was barely off the highway when she popped open her door, stuck her head out, and started heaving over the loose gravel on the shoulder of the road. She didn't throw up, as it turned out, but it was a close call. I sat quietly and waited for the spell to pass, knowing exactly how she felt. Seeing that car, it was like no time had passed at all. Ed had tried to tell me that we didn't know for absolute certain that it was her body, but really, who else could it be? It didn't seem possible—not for Tanya, the bright-eyed, blonde girl who had driven through the streets of Thistlewood in that lumbering green tank she'd bought with her wages from the diner, belting out Bonnie Tyler, Cyndi Lauper, and Pat Benatar at the top of her lungs. How had that girl, so full of promise and light, wound up at the bottom of the murky river?

Didn't seem possible. Definitely didn't seem fair.

And what gripped me the hardest was a thought that I couldn't put into words, not even to Wren. It was certainly possible that Tanya Blackburn had driven off that cliff on accident. But the far more likely scenario was that she had pressed her foot to the accelerator and sailed over the edge. Thelma without Louise.

If so, why? She hadn't seemed unhappy. Was there something she'd been hiding from us? Something she didn't think she could trust us with?

I was pretty sure Wren was thinking the same thing. But speaking the words would have made them real. So we both sat there, silent, as the sounds of early summer drifted in through the open door: wind, water trickling from an unseen stream, birds singing, and cicadas humming in the early afternoon air.

Closing my eyes, I tried to remove myself from my personal feelings and think about it as a reporter. The print version of the paper was delivered on Wednesdays, but the story would need to go up on the website as soon as possible. It wasn't going to be easy to write. I had to stay impartial. Stick to the facts and leave everything else for the gossips in town to sift through. And heavens knew, there would be plenty of them. I wouldn't report on the vanity plate or the identity of the person behind the wheel, even though I had no doubts in that regard. The remains had to be officially identified first, and even if I didn't care much for Tanya's mother, I wasn't going to publish that news until I knew that they'd been notified.

Wren shut the door and replaced her sunglasses on her face. "I'm sorry. I just had so many memories come rushing at me, all at once. Not just Tanya, but Jason being in the hospital, and knowing that I was headed off to basic training in three short weeks. Wondering if I'd made a mistake about enlisting. Good thing I skipped breakfast this morning, I guess."

"It's okay." I squeezed her hand, then gave her my phone. "We'll get through this. Could you call and ask Cassie to meet us over at the diner?"

"I'm *really* not hungry," she said.

"Me, either. But I need coffee to help me think."

☆ Chapter Four ☆

PAT'S DINER is a tourist magnet, with its neon lights, chrome ceiling, and booths with their own private juke-boxes. I wouldn't go so far as to call it a tourist *trap*, however, because the food is actually good and the prices are reasonable. The downside of that for year-round residents of Thistlewood is that it can be wicked hard to get a table once summer is in full swing. That was one reason I had Wren call Cassie as we were leaving the river—so that she could head over early to snag our usual booth.

The diner also holds a whole lot of memories for me and Wren, many of them bittersweet. Tanya had worked there our last two years of high school, so it was a rare day that we didn't at least stop in briefly to chat. Sometimes when I'm there, I can almost swear I hear her voice. And I'm almost certain that she was the last person in charge of updating the jukeboxes. The songs have always been mostly golden oldies, but they'd always drop a few low performers and add a couple of new hits to the mix every six months or so. There's not a single song on those jukeboxes that was recorded after 1987, however.

As we approached the diner, I began having second thoughts about whether this was a good idea. Maybe we should have gone to Wren's house, or to mine. But Cassie was waving to us, so I opened the door and we stepped inside. Patsy looked up when we entered, and I could tell from her expression she'd already heard something about the body. Which wasn't surprising. Her place is the central hub of Thistlewood's gossip grapevine.

I quickly glanced away, hoping to at least delay Patsy's barrage of questions. Cassie, I was glad to see, had already ordered lunch. I was doubly glad to see that she had finished what I was pretty sure was a fish and chips platter. Neither Wren nor I really needed to think much about fish after viewing the catch that the tow truck had just pulled in from the river.

"What happened?" Cassie asked as soon as Wren and I slipped into the booth. "You both sounded upset on the phone. Was it someone you knew?"

"Yeah," I answered in a shaky voice. "I recognized the car as soon as they pulled it—"

I stopped when Wren nudged my knee. Patsy was approaching.

"Well, look what the cat dragged in. I haven't seen either of you in a blue moon." Patsy Grimes is a walking stereotype of a middle-aged diner waitress, with teased bleached-blonde hair and a heavy coat of makeup. Think Flo from that old show *Alice*, but add fifty pounds and you'd be in the ballpark. I'd say her appearance was solely for the tourists, but she dresses exactly the same all year round. The only difference in the summer months is that she watches her language a bit more closely.

"Your memory must be going, Patsy," Wren said. "We were in here two days ago."

"Yeah, well, I've seen at least a hundred tourists since then," Patsy replied, popping her gum. " One in-season day around here is like seven the rest of the year. I swear I'm going to walk right out those doors one summer day and never come back."

I rolled my eyes. "That's a lie and you know it. You love this place."

"You got me there." She grinned. "But they've got two family reunions going on down at the campground, plus that biker group that's been coming over from Knoxville since—I don't know, maybe even back in the seventies. You've seen 'em, Wren. They used to be trouble. Started a fight here one time. But these days they're just a bunch of middle-aged coots parading around like they're Hell's Angels and stinking the place up with all that sweaty leather. Anyway, this is the first time I've had seats open all day, and I'm still short on help. You sure you ain't interested, Cassie? Tips are real good in the summer."

Cassie shook her head. "I tried waiting tables once.

I'm way too clumsy. By the time you subtracted for all the dishes I broke, I'd have to pay you to work here."

"Okay. Let me know if you change your mind." Patsy looked around to make sure no one was listening, then leaned forward to fill our coffee cups. "Is it true?" she asked, dropping her voice to a whisper.

My stomach clenched, even though I'd known she was going to ask as soon as I stepped in the door.

"Jesse and Mac were in here just a few minutes ago," Patsy continued when I didn't respond immediately. "Said some kids found a body in the river. Is that true or just more of his bullpucky?"

Jesse Yarnell is a regular, usually accompanied by his trusty sidekick, Mac, whose last name I can't remember. The two of them are by far the worst gossips in Thistlewood. Both are retired, and they park their well-padded behinds at the counter for at least a few hours a day during the off-season, trading barbs with Patsy, and occasionally her mom, Teresa. Patsy runs them off when the tourists are around because she needs the seating, and they rarely buy more than coffee and pie, or maybe breakfast. They also take ample advantage of the free coffee refills, not that I really have room to talk on that front. But I do think she misses the banter with Jesse when he's not around.

I debated just telling her I didn't know, but Patsy wouldn't believe me. She knew that if I hadn't already been down to the river to check things out for the paper, I'd at least have heard something about it from Ed, who would have heard from Billy Thorpe. So I'd have to give her some tidbit of information unless I wanted to end up on her bad side. And I really *didn't* want to be on Patsy's bad side. As someone who waited tables in college, I know better than to annoy anyone who has the power to surreptitiously spit in my soup. Not that I ever did that, or that I believed Patsy would, but why risk it?

So I didn't even bother with a lie. "It's true."

She heaved a sigh. "Dear Lord, it's only May. This town has already seen enough tragedy for a full year, what with that Edith Morton business. Do they know whose car it was?"

"Not yet." Technically, that wasn't a lie. *They* didn't know whose car it was. Wren and I, on the other hand, didn't have any doubt.

Patsy tapped the cap of her pen against her bottom lip. "Well, I hate it. Bad for business, and just a plain nasty way for anyone to go. So, ladies," she said, pasting on a weary version of her usual smile, "on that grim note, do you want to be happy or healthy today?"

That was Patsy's usual shorthand for whether we were ordering the barbecue bacon cheeseburger, which is sinfully good, or the soup and salad combo, which is decent but allows me to still zip my jeans without lying down on the bed and sucking in my breath.

"I think we're both just having coffee," Wren said. "This whole thing sort of zapped our appetite."

"Can't blame you there," Patsy said as she scooped

up Cassie's empty plate. "I'll be back with some more sweet tea for you in just a minute, hon."

"I'm good," Cassie told her.

"Okay, then. Wren, Ruth...just flag me down if y'all need a refill."

When Patsy breezed off to one of the other tables, I turned to Cassie and continued in a low voice. "It's Tanya Blackburn. I recognized the novelty plate, and also those weird headlights. It probably went over the edge at Lover's Leap, which is—"

"The second left past the bridge on River Road," Cassie said. "We spent summers here during high school, remember?"

"*O-kay*." I decided I really didn't want to inquire further on that point and looked out across the diner. There was a couple I didn't recognize on the other side, near the front. Tourists, most likely. The man took a quarter out of his pocket and popped it into the jukebox, and the woman leaned forward, poking at the numbers on the bottom. A few seconds later, a song crackled to life on the speakers, and soon Aretha Franklin was suggesting that we find out what "R-E-S-P-E-C-T" meant to her.

"You think about Tanya a lot," Cassie said. "I can tell, because it's usually when some eighties power ballad comes on. It always seemed weird to me that she just disappeared and no one bothered to look."

"Seemed weird to me, too," I told her.

"And they *claimed* they looked," Wren said. "It just didn't seem like they looked very hard."

I nodded. "Exactly. Her car was gone. Her clothes were gone. She was eighteen. Her parents told the cops she had been talking about leaving for years. And that was true. But we were leaving together. She might not have told *them* if she was leaving..."

"But she would have told us," Wren finished. "And I think she might have told her brother, too. She and Bud had grown apart a bit, and he annoyed her as much as James annoyed me sometimes, but they still took care of each other. Sally Blackburn was always off doing something with her church or some social thing either here or over in Maryville where Tanya's aunt lived. The kids sort of fended for themselves."

"Kind of surprised that Bud is living with his mom. Is she in bad health?"

"I don't think so," Wren said. "I still see her downtown. Bud, though...I don't know what happened to him. He seemed bright enough in school. I think he got into drugs when he lived outside Thistlewood. After he came home, he seemed a little off. I think he did odd jobs with his dad's construction firm for a while. And he still does handyman stuff. His flyer is over there on the bulletin board." She nodded at the community board near the door, just above the rack that holds copies of the *Thistlewood Star*. "Nothing steady, though, as far as I know. Back when I was interning at Memory Grove, the old owner hired Bud to paint the reception area. He did a good job, but he seemed kind of...dazed." She gave a little laugh. "He nearly fell off the ladder when he realized who I was. Pretty sure he never, ever believed I'd come back to Thistlewood."

"And he was not alone on that count," I said.

"True. You could definitely have put me in the *never-ever* category when I left. But things change, as we both know. And yeah, Bud probably felt like Tanya abandoned him, leaving all of a sudden like that. It must have hurt."

I thought back to that night on the stairs. "You're right. Mrs. Blackburn mostly seemed angry when she sent me back to check out Tanya's room. The clothes were all gone. Nothing there but her song notebook, the one thing she definitely wouldn't have left. But when I saw Bud in the hallway, he seemed sad. Kind of deflated, like he'd lost all of his energy."

We were silent for a moment, then Cassie said, "I'm so sorry. It had to have been awful seeing that car emerge from the river. Are the two of you okay?"

I gave her a tiny smile. "Yeah. I think we're mostly in shock."

"Do you think..." Cassie looked uncomfortable, and I was pretty sure I knew where this was headed. "You said the car went off at Lover's Leap. Do you think maybe there was a guy she was in love with? Someone who rejected her? Maybe she did a Thelma and Louise over the side, like in that movie? Only...without Louise."

"Well, that's proof positive that you are my daughter.

I had that very same thought on the drive back. But I don't think so."

"What changed your mind?" Wren asked.

"Remember what I told you about Mrs. Blackburn sending me back to check out Tanya's room?"

They both nodded, and then Cassie said, "Ah. The clothes. If you were planning to make a dramatic exit like that, would you pack your clothes?"

Wren's eyes widened. "Come to think of it, why would you pack *all* of your clothes, even if you were running off? Tanya had stuff in that closet she hadn't worn since fifth grade."

That was an excellent point, and I mentally kicked myself for not thinking of it thirty-two years ago. Maybe there was someone at the sheriff's office who would have listened if I'd presented them with that bit of logic. If nothing else, I might have been able to convince my boss at the *Star*. Jim Dealey had printed an article about Tanya's disappearance, even continued to run a notice for a few months after I left for college. But I'd always had the sense it was simply because he knew how sad I was about her disappearance. Like pretty much everyone else in town, he'd believed her parents.

Aretha's last *sock it to me* faded out, and the opening bars of the couple's second jukebox selection began.

Wren turned to look at me. "You gotta be kidding."

The three of us sat there, silent, as Bonnie Tyler's "Total Eclipse of the Heart" battled with the sounds of dishes clattering, laughter from a booth with four teens (one of whom I'm fairly certain was Ed's niece, Kate), and a baby crying. I suspected that there would be a service of some sort for Tanya, once her remains were officially identified. But this—her favorite song playing here in the diner where she'd worked—was Tanya Blackburn's real memorial.

Chapter Five

THE SONG ENDED, and Wren and I debated a second cup of coffee. Then Cassie's head turned toward the door and very quickly turned back. She grabbed the dessert menu from the holder on the condiment tray and began to scan it. I glanced up at the chrome ceiling to figure out who she'd spotted. Ah-ha. Dean Jacobs had just walked in.

Was she trying to *avoid* him by hiding behind the menu? Or simply trying to look nonchalant? I was almost certain it was the latter, so I waved. Dean waved back and headed our way.

"*Mom*," she hissed, "I was trying to play it cool."

Wren laughed and whispered, "Too late."

Dean was apparently off duty now, because he'd changed into jeans and a dark-blue polo shirt that matched his eyes. The tip of a tattoo peeked out from the collar of his shirt. I wasn't sure how I felt about that, but I knew my daughter would consider it a major plus. Cassie could show him the heart on her ankle and the flower on her arm—both small and tasteful, but the appeal of inking up mystified me. She'd told me I should get a star tattoo right after I bought the *Star*. But that wasn't happening, and she knew it. I had to force myself to get a flu shot every year, so there was no way I'd voluntarily go anywhere near a needle.

"We meet again," Dean said. "But it looks like y'all are finishing up."

"Nope." Cassie slid over to make room in the booth. "We were actually about to order *pie*." The look that she gave me and Wren made it clear we would be staying at least a little bit longer. And, apparently, we would be eating pie.

A crash came from behind the counter, followed by a few choice words from Patsy, each one of which would have required a hefty deposit into the swear jar if she'd had such a thing. One of the teenaged boys who was sitting at the booth across from us laughed and gave her a round of applause.

"Sorry!" Patsy glanced around, breathing a sigh of relief when she realized that there were no small children in the dining room. "I do try to rein it in once tourist season starts," she told the two teens. "But sometimes I slip up. Guess y'all will have to be honorary citizens of Thistlewood."

"Nothing we haven't heard before, right, Jack?" The older one grinned at the kid opposite him, almost certainly his brother, who was wearing a T-shirt with *Buckeye Nation* across the front. The younger boy seemed preoccupied. He just gave Patsy a weak smile and went back to flipping through the songs on the jukebox.

When Patsy eventually made it back to our table, Dean ordered something called a Lumberjack Breakfast —pancakes, choice of meat, eggs, biscuits, and gravy.

"Scrambled or fried, hon? And did you want sausage, bacon, or country ham?"

Just listening to Patsy walk him through the options caused my cholesterol to rise a few points. Looking at Dean, I wondered where he could possibly put it. The guy was thin as a whip, but then, he did most of his deliveries on foot. He always said it was quicker that way, which is definitely the case during the summer months when tourists coming through on their way to the river can clog Main Street from one end of town to the other.

Per Cassie's orders, the rest of us had pie. Wren looked like even her slice of key lime was pushing the envelope a bit, but I was actually feeling a little better. Hearing Tanya's favorite song—the one she always called her *theme song*—had been cathartic. I took a bite of peach pie and thought about the many times we had sat in this very booth all those years ago, sometimes with Tanya, but even more often with her in the waitress uniform, taking our order and then sneaking back to chat with us between customers.

Dean looked like he was trying to work up the

courage to say something. Finally, he turned to Cassie and said, "I'm glad that you're here. I've been thinking about what you said earlier in the mail truck, and I have a proposition."

Cassie raised an eyebrow. "Oh?"

Wren and I exchanged a smile. What exactly had the two of them talked about on the ride back from the estate sale?

Dean, who'd clearly caught our exchange, flushed. "Um...a *business* proposition? You said you were looking for a job. And I haven't mentioned this to anyone yet, because it's still in the planning phase, but I'm opening a business in the old antique store building."

"Really?" I said. "That's just a few doors down from the *Star*. I saw some contractors there the other day and asked Patsy what was going on. For once, she didn't have a clue."

"Yeah," Dean replied. "I'm trying to keep it on the down low. The place has been vacant for a couple of years, so I'm getting a pretty good deal. And it's a cool space. The upstairs is huge, completely open. I've saved up a bit, and also have a little money that my grandmother left to me. It's a little risky, I guess, but as the old saying goes, *nothing ventured, nothing gained.*"

"What kind of business?" Wren asked.

"A bookstore. There's no place in town that sells books. We could even have signings if you happen to know any local authors who might be willing." He wagged his eyebrows up and down.

"I'm pretty sure that could be arranged," I told him, since I couldn't imagine Ed saying no.

Dean glanced over his shoulder to make sure Patsy wasn't within earshot, and then added in a lower voice, "I also want to put in a coffee shop downstairs. Personally, I like the diner's coffee just fine, but you have no idea how many tourists stop me to ask for directions to the nearest Starbucks when they're craving their mocha frappalatte-whatevers."

Cassie chuckled. "I can believe it. It was a culture shock to me when I came here. In Nashville, you can't swing a cat without hitting at least one."

"Exactly. So, I'm putting in a coffee bar. We'd sell little trinkets, too. Souvenirs. Hopefully, handmade items from people in town who make jewelry and so forth. The upstairs area would be separate, though, and this is the part that some people are going to think is kind of out there. I want to turn it into a gaming cafe."

"Like, arcade games?" I asked.

Apparently I had just shown my age because Dean and Cassie exchanged an amused glance.

"I *might* put in some arcade games," he said reluctantly. "But more like esports. Gaming computers where you can play games like *Fortnite* and *Overwatch*. *League of Legends*. Stuff like that. I think it would be a big hit during the tourist season, when kids—and adults, too—get dragged away from their computers and game consoles to come camping. A day or two of that, and they're in withdrawal, just like the ones needing their Starbucks fix. I think they'd be willing to fork over twenty bucks to play on a decent machine for a few hours. And it might help keep the place profitable off-season, too, as long as I lower the rates a bit for locals. There's nowhere in Thistlewood for kids to hang out after school or on the weekends."

I thought that Patsy might beg to differ on that point, but to be honest, there really wasn't much for them to *do* here, aside from eating and listening to old songs on the jukebox.

"Wouldn't that be kind of noisy, though, with all those games going on?" Wren asked. "I mean, bookstores are usually quiet."

Dean grinned. "They use headphones, although there might be the occasional loud *whoop* when someone wins a match. And I'm guessing most of our traffic upstairs will be at night. But I am planning on doing some soundproofing. That's probably what Ruth saw the other day."

Cassie turned in the booth so that she was facing Dean. "So...where do I come in?"

"Well, I'm hoping you'd manage the place. I'll still work with the post office, so I'd only be there part-time. And to be honest, I don't know a whole lot about running a business. I was dreading the whole process of hiring someone. When you said today that you helped run the store you worked at in Nashville, it was like the clouds parted and delivered a miracle."

Cassie laughed. "You're thinking of hiring me to run

a coffee bar? I've never even touched an espresso machine, so you might want to reconsider that whole miracle thing. How many employees would we have?"

Dean smiled, and his entire face lit up like a Christmas tree. I think it might have been her casual use of the word *we*, which made it clear that she was giving his proposition serious consideration.

"Just you at first," Dean said. "Although we may need to pull in a teenager to help during the season, especially with the gaming section."

Cassie looked across the table. I could tell from her startled expression that she'd pretty much forgotten Wren and I were even here. The light in her eyes dimmed, and I knew she was remembering about Tanya. Maybe feeling a little guilty about being excited about this when we were still feeling bruised. That was silly, though. We weren't even supposed to be talking about it to anyone yet. And unlike Patsy, Dean didn't seem to have his ears to the grapevine.

Dean must have noticed Cassie's change of mood, because he quickly added, "You don't have to answer right now. Just think about it, okay?"

I reached across the table and squeezed Cassie's hand. "It sounds like it's right up your alley, hon."

Wren agreed. "If you're going to stay in Thistlewood, I doubt you'll find anything else that would be as perfect for you. *And* I just realized that I need to take off." She pushed her partially eaten pie aside. "The two of you talking about books reminded me that I still need to pick up the ones I bought at the estate sale."

I told Wren that I'd cover her pie and coffee, and once she was gone, I said, "I really need to get back to work, too. Just take the Jeep home. You can pick me up later or I'll catch a ride with Ed."

Patsy arrived with the four plates that contained Dean's cholesterol extravaganza and, at my request, fished my check out of her apron pocket. As I headed off to the cash register, Cassie and Dean were already talking about the new venture again, and I smiled. I hadn't seen her that excited about anything in a long time, even though she was trying to play it a little bit cool in front of Dean.

As usual, there was a line at the register. An elderly couple was just finishing up, and the two brothers I'd noticed earlier were ahead of me. The younger one was looking at something on his phone, which reminded me that I might as well check my emails while I was waiting.

"Do not text her, Jack," the older boy said. "I'm serious. They probably just got to Cherokee, and we're not going to hear the end of it from Dad and Aunt Carrie if they have to turn around and come back to deal with this."

"I just keep seeing it," the younger one said as they paid their bill.

The logo on his T-shirt clicked then. *Buckeye Nation. Ohio State.* Ed had said that the boys were from

Ohio, and I had a good idea what it was the kid couldn't stop seeing.

I walked back over to our booth and handed the check to Cassie, along with some cash. "Can you take care of this please? I need to run."

And I kind of did need to run, since they were already heading out the door toward the parking lot.

"Hey," I called out. "Wait up!"

They turned around, and the older one frowned. "What? We already paid. I even left a tip."

"No. I don't work here." I held out my hand. "I'm Ruth Townsend."

"Rich Smith," he said, ignoring my hand. "This is Jack."

Pulling my hand back down to my side, I said, "I own the newspaper here in town. The *Thistlewood Star*. I was just down at the river, and then I couldn't help but over-hear you two talking a moment ago—"

Rich's frown turned into an all-out scowl. "*No comment.* We're not talking to you."

"Please, it'll just take a minute." I gave him my best smile, but it didn't make a dent. Mentioning that I was a reporter had clearly been a mistake.

Rich opened the driver's-side door of his truck and got in. "We already gave our story to the sheriff, and we're not repeating it. Get in, Jack."

Jack opened the door as his brother started the truck. The engine was loud, and I had to yell to be heard over the roar. "I knew her, okay? She was my friend."

When his younger brother hesitated, Rich said, "C'mon, Jack. Now."

Jack did as he was told, and they roared out of the parking lot, kicking up a fine spray of dust and gravel in their wake.

Well, I thought, *that could have gone better.*

☆ Chapter Six ☆

I'D JUST UPLOADED the pictures I took at the river to the images folder at the *Star*'s website when I glanced up and saw Steve Blevins in dark aviator sunglasses, watching me through the plate-glass window of the *Star*'s front office. I cocked my head to one side and stared back until he opened the door and stepped inside.

"Townsend," he said.

"Blevins," I replied. "Are you here for a reason or just trying to brighten up my day with your sparkling personality and witty conversation?"

I was glad that the images were on the server now, since I was a little worried that Blevins might demand my camera, and maybe even my computer. That would be illegal, and I'd eventually get them back, but I really didn't want to go through the hassle of hauling the county sheriff into court.

Blevins took his sunglasses off, and I expected to see

his trademark smirk. But he looked exhausted. His eyes were red, and while it might have been due to allergies, I was pretty sure he'd been crying. As much as I disliked the man, I felt bad for not realizing that finding Tanya in that car couldn't have been easy for him, either. The Blevins family was definitely *from-here*. Our senior yearbook had included a kindergarten classroom photo from the mid-seventies with thirty-five bright, shiny *from-here* faces. Steve Blevins had been one of those faces. So had Tanya Blackburn. He might not have been as close to her in high school as Wren and I were, but he'd known her much longer. Probably even had a crush on her, since pretty much every guy I knew at Thistlewood High had been crushing on her at some point.

Something in my expression must have shifted. Blevins looked away, seemingly uncomfortable with his vulnerability. In search of a distraction, his eyes fell on the box leaning against the brick wall.

"What's that?" he asked.

"Just some artwork I bought this morning at Lucy McBride's estate sale." That wasn't entirely true, since Cassie hadn't been able to convince Kenneth to take my money. She said he'd seemed a little confused, but he insisted that his mom must have meant for me to have the paintings if my name was on the box.

"They any good?" Blevins asked.

"I bought them, didn't I?"

He gave a little point-taken nod, then sat down in the chair across from my desk. I really didn't want to be petty, but that was Ed's chair. When Ed visits, he heads straight for that chair, because my office is the last stop on the daily walk that he takes, rain or shine. He's hurting by the time he gets here, and he sinks down into that chair with a major sigh of relief. And there's little doubt in Ed's mind that the person who put that hurt on him was Derrick Blevins, Steve's then seventeen-year-old son. But family members had circled the wagons around the kid, including Blevins's father-in-law, who was a county judge. Derrick had an ironclad alibi. Couldn't have been him, or so they claimed.

"What do you want, Steve? It must be something. You're not in the habit of just dropping by to shoot the breeze. If it's about the pictures I took, I already told you. I'm not going to publish anything inappropriate."

His shoulders slumped. "I know, okay? It ain't about that. I need to ask you a favor."

I didn't say anything. Just looked at him, waiting for him to go on. And yes, I was kind of enjoying his discomfort. It was petty, perhaps, but back in high school, Blevins had been the kind of guy who—despite having a cool car and good hair—had to ask a freshman girl to senior prom because the girls his own age were tired of him bragging about sexual conquests, most of which we knew hadn't happened. One of which I *personally* knew for an absolute fact hadn't happened. I guess he still had the *cool car* in a way, since he was the only one in the county who had *SHERIFF* on the side in big green letters and he could pull over any driver he wanted on the slimmest of pretexts. Time and karma had taken care of the *good-hair* situation, however, which is why you rarely see him without a hat.

After a full twenty seconds of uncomfortable silence, he sighed. "Look, I'll just get right down to it."

"Please do."

"Someone needs to tell Tanya Blackburn's family that we found her car and we *might* have found her remains. I stress *might* have because we don't know for sure. There's a bit of a...complication."

"What sort of complication?"

"A complication that I can't explain right now," he continued. "But that's the angle this *someone* needs to approach this from—we *might* have found her body."

"And why on God's green earth do you think that someone should be me?"

He shrugged. "You were her best friend."

"One of them," I said. "Given Wren's line of work..."

"Wren's line of work is precisely *why* I'm not asking her."

Okay, he had a point there. If you're going with the whole we-don't-know-for-certain angle, Wren shouldn't be involved. Funeral directors are generally only involved once you know. I suspected, however, that there were other reasons for his dismissal of Wren.

"Why can't *you* tell them, Steve?" I sat back in my chair, the leather blessedly cool against my bare neck. "Isn't that part of your job?"

"Yes. But you remember Bud, right?"

"Tanya's brother. Of course I do."

"Well, I've arrested him a few times. Mostly drunk and disorderly. Nothing too major...at least not yet. Needless to say, though, the family doesn't care for me much." He gave a short bark of laughter. "I'm not even sure they would open the door if they saw me coming up the driveway."

"And you think they'll open it for me? I'm a reporter."

"But you"—he corrected with a point of his sunglasses—"are also a family friend."

That was stretching things more than a little. "I was *Tanya's* friend." I cleared my throat. "When Tanya went missing, I had a falling out with her mom."

"Why?" Blevins seemed genuinely interested, which struck me as odd. He'd never been the curious type, which was one reason, according to Ed, that Blevins was a lousy deputy and an even worse sheriff.

"Because I was the only one, aside from Wren, who questioned their nonsense explanation that Tanya had skipped town. Everyone else just nodded their heads and bought the lie."

"Well, there was a reason for that. You hadn't known her as long as most of us. Maybe you didn't realize that Tanya had been talking about leaving Thistlewood since elementary school. She was going to—"

"Nashville. Yeah, Steve. No duh. Tanya and I had been going through classified ads in the *Nashville News-Journal* for months, looking for apartments close to

Vanderbilt. But leaving that aside, why would Tanya take her clothes but not her songwriting notebook? Why pack all of her clothes, even the ones she'd outgrown years ago?"

He looked a little surprised at that, and I again mentally kicked myself for not realizing this thirty-two years ago. The sheriff back then, according to Ed, had been smarter than Blevins.

"So yeah, I didn't buy it," I continued. "But no one listened."

"Okay. Okay, I get it." Blevins dropped his hands into his lap. "But would you please do this for me, Ruth? I'm asking nicely."

I almost laughed, and I guess he could tell he was losing traction, because he quickly shifted to a different strategy.

"Fine. Do it for Tanya, then. Do you really want the news getting back to her family next time they walk into the diner, or on freaking Facebook, for crying out loud?"

He had a point. I also didn't want them finding out from the article and photos I'd be publishing online shortly. I sighed. So did Blevins, but he knew he had won.

"When?"

"It needs to be soon," he said. "We're trying to keep everything as quiet as possible. I haven't even let them haul the car to the impound lot yet. There's no way to get there without going through town, and Tanya's plate on the front was...unique."

"It's also removable."

"Not after thirty-two years at the bottom of Freedom River." He started for the door. "I owe you one, Ruthie—"

I'm pretty sure he was about to add the word *baby*. That was his standard snarky name for me back in the day...*Ruthie baby* or that tired old standby, *Babe Ruth*. Luckily for him, he caught himself in time because I was already reaching for the stapler on my desk and wondering if I could throw it hard enough to hit him in the back of the head before the door closed. I mean, it wasn't as if he could arrest me.

Not if he wanted me to do him a favor.

After he left, I reluctantly closed the laptop and flipped the sign on the office door to *closed*. It was only about a ten-minute walk from here to the Blackburn house. I had to walk past Wren's Memory Grove Funeral Home to get there. If she was looking out the window, she'd probably wonder why I didn't stop. But I knew that if I did stop, she'd probably say this wasn't something I should have to do on my own. And I'd have been sorely tempted to let her come along, since I really, really didn't want to do this.

When I reached the Blackburn house, I walked up the stone pathway and raised my hand to knock on the blue door, just as I'd done so many times as a teenager. My knuckles were about to make contact when the door was suddenly yanked open.

The change in Sally Blackburn was breathtaking.

Her hair, always wrapped in a tight bun behind her head, was almost entirely gray now, and her face was heavily lined, especially around her mouth. I thought it very likely that she'd taken up smoking over the past three decades.

"Mrs. Blackburn," I said, "it's Ruth Townsend."

She rolled her eyes. "I know who you are, Ruth. I may be old, but my mind is still sharp. What do you want?"

I took a deep breath of the hot, muggy air. "I just need to speak with you for a moment. Won't take long."

She stepped aside. "Come on in, then. No point in me air-conditioning the whole dang neighborhood while you speak your piece."

Entering the Blackburn house was like stepping through a time machine. Nothing, as far as I could tell, had changed, aside from the lighting. It seemed much dimmer than I remembered, but that was probably because the curtains were drawn, despite the fact that it was a bright sunny day. Two rather wimpy lamps burned on either side of the living room sofa, which separated the living room and dining room. I stopped and placed my hand on the floral print fabric. I could be wrong, but I'd swear it was the very same couch.

When I closed my eyes, I saw Tanya. We'd been goofing around one day when I'd stayed over. I'd been sitting sideways on the couch with my feet up. She came running downstairs and flipped over the back of the sofa, intending to end up next to me. But she'd pushed off a little too hard. Her bottom skidded off the cushion, and she'd landed on the carpet with a soft thud and a scream of laughter.

I opened my eyes and blinked away tears. Mrs. Blackburn was now seated on the sofa, in the same spot I'd been all those years ago. It was all a little too much, and for a moment, I just stood there, swaying on my feet.

"Don't just stand there. Sit down."

The words were congenial enough, but the tone wasn't friendly in the slightest.

"This is about Tanya, isn't it?" she said as soon as I sat at the opposite end of the couch. "I can't think of any other reason you'd be here. Going to do a story on her? See if there are any more skeletons in people's closets you can unearth like you did with Edie Morton?" She raised her eyebrows sarcastically at me.

I ignored the jab and asked, "Is Bud here, Mrs. Blackburn?"

"It's Sally," she said, waving her hand dismissively in the air. "If I think there's something Bud needs to hear, I'll be sure to pass it along. So whatever you've got to say, spit it out."

What *was* it with mothers in this town trying to control their full-grown sons' lives? I was tempted to remind her that if Edith had let Clarence out from under her thumb a bit, the skeletons she'd been hiding might have stayed safely buried. She might even still be alive. But I suspected that Mrs. Blackburn wouldn't appreciate my unsolicited advice.

Fine, then. I would do as I was told. I would just *spit it out*.

"Tanya's car was found in the river today."

Sally Blackburn's expression didn't change, but her entire body went rigid. Her hands were white and clenched next to her on the sofa.

"Where?" she croaked.

"Down near Jolly's Marina. A couple of teenagers were snorkeling, and they found the car. It's definitely her car. I recognized the novelty tag."

"*B TYLER*," she said absently.

I nodded. "But they haven't identified the body yet. They're taking the remains to a lab in Knoxville to be identified. The car is definitely hers, but it might not...*be* her."

As much as I tried to sound hopeful, the words sounded utterly ridiculous, especially coming from me. I was the one who had been worried all those years ago, that something like this had happened. Who had refused to believe the happy little fiction that Mrs. Blackburn tried to sell me.

The woman was completely silent, staring at something invisible on the carpet. A good thirty seconds ticked by, while I waited for her to say or do something. She looked brittle, and I had the strangest sense that anything I said might shatter her into a million jagged bits.

Finally, when I simply couldn't bear the silence any longer, I said, "Are you okay, Mrs. Blackburn?"

"It's *Sally*," she screamed, leaping to her feet. "Sally. Sally. Sally."

She was right in my face, screaming. I leaned away from the onslaught, actually worried for a moment that I was going to have to physically defend myself against a woman in her seventies.

But the wind seemed to be fading from her sails rather quickly. "You need to leave," she said in a much lower voice. "Get out of here. Please. Just go."

"I'm sorry," I said. "Sheriff Blevins thought it would be better if I told you."

Sally laughed bitterly. "What on earth gave him that fool-headed idea?"

As I turned to go, I saw a man on the stairs. At first, I thought it was Mr. Blackburn, because the guy looked too old to be only forty-eight. But judging from what Wren and Blevins had said, Bud Blackburn had been living pretty hard for the past few decades. And even as bloodshot as they were now, his eyes were unmistakable. They wore the same sad expression they had the night his mother had sent me upstairs to inspect Tanya's totally empty closet.

"Hey, Ruth," he said with a shy smile. "I heard you were back in town." He moved across the small foyer quickly and hugged me. Awkwardly, I returned the gesture, trying hard not to wrinkle my nose. His clothes smelled sour, like they'd been left in the washer for days on end. There were flecks of something on his shirt. Purple and black. Paint, most likely. Wren had said he did handyman work, so maybe he just hadn't changed out of his work clothes yet...or ever.

Okay, that wasn't nice, but the guy desperately needed a shower.

"It's good to see you, Bud," I said, gently pulling away from his embrace. I had always liked him, even though he was still in the annoying-little-brother stage when Tanya and I first became friends. Later, though, he'd generally left us alone. He'd yell down into the basement sometimes and ask if we wanted popcorn. And he'd occasionally come down to watch a movie we'd rented. *The Goonies. Ferris Bueller.* Otherwise, we didn't see much of him. He cut lawns for two entire summers so he could buy a motorcycle when he was fifteen, and generally ran with a different crowd. An older, rougher crowd, for the most part. I'd had the sense Tanya wasn't exactly happy with his choices in that regard. But it was probably kind of tough living in her shadow.

Mrs. Blackburn—and I would never, ever be able to think of her as Sally, no matter how many times she screamed the name at me—moved around the side of the couch. For a moment, I'd forgotten she was even in the room.

"Ruth was just leaving. She's going back to her office now to write up a real nice story about Tanya for the paper. Because they found her car. In the river. Her body was in it. I'm going to make iced tea now."

Without another word, she turned on her heel and headed for the kitchen. That was probably a good thing, since I would have had the urge to smack her if she'd still been within reach. How could she have been so callous as to just drop the news on the poor guy like that?

Bud stood frozen, watching his mother's retreating back.

"I'm sorry, Bud. But she's right. They found Tanya's car this morning in the river. A driver was at the wheel, and...they *think* it's her. But they don't know for sure yet."

He stumbled backward, and for a moment, I was terrified he was going to pass out. Instead, he sat down heavily on the bottom step.

I sat down next to Bud and squeezed his hand. He still smelled like moldy laundry, but all I could see was the gangly boy who'd brought down a bowl of popcorn and plopped onto the beanbag to watch *Teen Wolf* with us. Who, despite their typical sibling squabbles, had loved his sister.

"I'm sorry you had to find out that way, Bud. I really am."

"So am I," he said. "But...you'd probably better go now. You know what she's like."

I nodded. "I'll let you know if I hear anything else. Calls to the *Star* transfer to my cell if I'm not there. Call if you need anything, okay?"

☆ Chapter Seven ☆

CASSIE CRACKED the sliding glass door and stuck her head through. "You want pepper jack or Gouda, Mom? And a toasted bun?"

I debated for a moment. "Pepper jack. And definitely toasted."

She and Ed were out on the deck grilling burgers while I made a chopped salad. As she closed the door, Cassie laughed at a comment from Ed. I couldn't make out what he'd said over the sound of the faucet as I rinsed the vegetables, but I smiled at the sight of them. Ed was quickly becoming an integral part of our day-to-day life in Thistlewood—more so than I would ever have imagined a few months before when we met at his book signing. I didn't know where our relationship was headed, but a day with Ed in it was always brighter, and it warmed my heart that the two of them were getting along so well.

That hadn't always been the case with Cassie and her father. She loved Joe, and vice versa, but once she'd hit the age where she had her own opinions and interests, their relationship had begun to show signs of stress. Joe seemed to think that kids were these malleable creatures that you could shape into your own image. But Cassie had always been her own person, and instead of celebrating that, he'd spent most of their time together trying to change her. Joe had wanted Cassie to play baseball as a kid, and she gave it a try, but she'd had a strong preference for soccer. He'd bought her a dirt bike, but she really wasn't a daredevil and was more comfortable riding on sidewalks. He'd agreed to pay for college, but only if she chose a "practical" major, which for him meant business or nursing. He and I argued about that. I'd eventually won, partly because I pointed out that most of the contributions to her college account had come from my salary, not his. And the point had been moot since Cassie had dropped out after a year, saying she wasn't really ready yet.

The divorce had strained their relationship even further. I hated that, but there wasn't much I could do to change it. Cassie said she'd kind of felt like he ran me out of town, and I wondered if that wasn't part of the reason she'd decided not to go back to Nashville. Had she felt that living there, four hours away, was somehow taking his side over mine?

I hoped not. It wasn't true that he'd run me off. I could have stayed in Nashville. I could have fought him

for the house. Could have found another job there, something to keep me busy after taking the offer of early
retirement from my old employer, the *Nashville News-
Journal,* when they had a round of cutbacks. Life would
have eventually felt normal again. But Cassie had
seemed happy in Nashville, content with her circle of
friends, a job she enjoyed, and two roommates that she
alternately loved to pieces and wanted to strangle. I'd
had the cabin here in Thistlewood. Wren was here and
so was the *Star,* which had been shuttered after Mr.
Dealey died. The paper had desperately needed
someone willing to breathe new life into it, and I'd
desperately needed a project. And Ed had been here,
although I hadn't known that would be an important
factor at the time.

With the late afternoon sun glinting off the purple
highlights in her dark hair, there was no escaping the fact
that Cassie looked far more like the tourists, many of
whom came from places like Nashville, than a Thistlewood native. Anyone would guess that she was not *from
here.* But maybe that didn't matter so much once you
were out of the crucible of high school. Cassie seemed
happy here. She'd even mused about taking some college
courses again, either in Knoxville or online. And now it
sounded like she might have found a job that would chal-
lenge her.

Still, I couldn't help but wonder if she'd felt like I
was abandoning her when I moved to Thistlewood. My
thoughts flashed back to Bud Blackburn's face—the

younger Bud, in the hallway that night thirty-two years ago. Looking like he was all alone. And, of course, that brought my mind right back to finding Tanya's car, which was the very thing I'd been trying *not* to think about.

I'd posted the article online moments before Ed arrived to drive me home from the office. It was brief and vague. *Breaking news. Police investigating.* Nothing about Tanya or the make of the car. Just the location where it was found and the fact that divers had located it, along with a murky photograph of the tow truck with the chain vanishing into the river. I didn't even mention that the divers were tourists.

A comment had popped up at almost the same instant that the little bell above the door had jingled, signaling Ed's arrival. Just someone asking if there were more details yet, which was kind of ridiculous since I'd posted the story less than five minutes earlier. I'd stared at the comment with very mixed feelings. Yes, it was kind of cool to see that someone had actually signed up for the *Star's* local news alerts feature. On the other hand, by the time there were two or three people posting, there was a very good chance that the discussion thread would devolve into sheer gossip.

I'd been wanting to check the story since we walked in the door, but I held off, not wanting to seem like I was obsessing. The salad was made now, however, and Ed and Cassie seemed to have the burger situation well in hand, so I decided it was as good a time as any to go upstairs to my computer and check the activity on the site.

Sure enough, there were new comments. Seven of them now. No one had any additional information to offer, but they were all eager to speculate. One said the car belonged to the former mayor, who vanished about ten years back. Another claimed that he or she had seen the car, and it had out-of-state tags. Someone else said she'd heard it was a station wagon and there was an entire family inside. The most outrageous of the responses speculated, without any sort of evidence or explanation, that the vehicle was an ice-cream truck.

And one said there was a body in the trunk.

That settled it. I logged in to the admin screen, scrolled down, and disabled the comments section, something I'd never done in the past. While I firmly believe that people have the right to voice their opinions—whatever they may be, and no matter how ill-informed they may be—about news stories, I had no intention of allowing the *Star*'s webpage to become host to a tangled mess of gossip and lies. Maybe once we had all of the facts, I'd change the setting, but for now, this story was a one-way street.

I set the laptop back on my nightstand and went to the window. Outside, the sun was going down, and the wide Tennessee sky was alive with a fireworks show of deep red and vibrant orange. The mountains glimmered in this pulsing glow. I felt myself relaxing a bit for the first time since we left the river. Then I thought of Tanya and how she had been waiting all those years for someone to find her car, and the calming effect of the beautiful May sunset outside began to slip.

Stop it, Tanya's voice said inside my head. *I wasn't waiting. I moved on long ago, Ruth. You know that.*

And I really *didn't* think she'd been waiting. All that they pulled out of the river today was her car and whatever remained of her body. The thing that made her Tanya had moved on thirty-two years ago.

But knowing *where* Tanya ended up still left so many questions wide open. I needed closure. So did Wren, and so did Tanya's brother. And we'd never get that until we knew *how* Tanya's car wound up at the bottom of the river. I had given up thirty-two years ago because I was fresh out of high school and no one, not even Mr. Dealey, had really believed me. That wouldn't happen again. This time, I wouldn't let her down.

I pushed the curtains all the way open to let the last light of the sunset in and told the little smart speaker next to my bed to play something by Bonnie Tyler. A smile spread across my face as "Holding Out for a Hero" began.

The hardwood floor was warm against my bare feet. I closed my eyes. It was sophomore year again, and I was dancing in the basement with Tanya and Wren. Moving through the room to the beat of our then-favorite song. Happy. Laughing. Being a bit too silly, but we were fifteen and had our whole lives stretched out in front of us.

I moved to the music, trying to recapture just a bit of that feeling. And for a few minutes, I did.

When the song ended, I opened my eyes and found Cassie standing in my open doorway.

"Supper is ready," she said with a smile.

I brushed a strand of hair out of my now-flushed face. "Be right down."

Cassie started toward the stairs, then leaned back inside and gave me a thumbs-up. "Not half bad for fifty. Go Mom."

☆ Chapter Eight ☆

I RARELY WORK ON SUNDAYS, especially now that Cassie has moved in with me. My usual pattern is a half day on Saturday, and then I take the rest of the weekend off, maybe working a little from home. But the previous day hadn't been a normal Saturday, and I had way too much pent-up energy on Sunday morning to just putter around the house. I'd taken the binoculars onto the deck with my cat, Cronkite, and tried some bird-watching therapy. It's usually pretty effective for getting my head to a happy place. But even though I'd spotted a goldfinch —one of my favorites—I'd been too jittery to sit still for long. So I'd jotted a note to Cassie, poured some extra coffee into a travel mug to be sure I wouldn't have to fight the brunch crowd at the diner, and was behind my desk by a quarter of eight.

My main goal for the day was to get a more detailed

article written so that when the ID came back positive, as I was sure it would, I'd have all of my ducks in a row, along with some ideas about where to begin my investigation. The *Star*'s morgue, which is reporter lingo for the room where all the past editions are shelved, was my first stop. I'd never particularly liked hanging out in the morgue, partly because it was called *the morgue* and I have a morbid imagination, but mostly because it was dimly lit and dusty. Cleaning it didn't help much because most of the dust was from slowly degrading newspapers.

Shelves that resembled giant mail slots lined two walls of the room. There were forty-eight in all—eight rows of six. One hundred and seventeen binders were stored here, one for each year since the *Star* began publication. Five of the binders were empty, since the *Star* had been closed between the time Mr. Dealey died and my relaunch of the paper the previous January. I'd felt a little silly writing the year on the spine of binders that would never be filled. But one day I'd like to pull together at least a rudimentary overview of key events during that time from papers in neighboring towns and from the memories of those who lived here, so that the paper can serve as a relatively uninterrupted historical archive for Thistlewood.

A fine lattice of cobwebs covered the opening like an early winter frost. I cleared it away, removed the 1987 binder, and placed it on the worktable in the corner. An odd sense of déjà vu hit me as I looked at two sheets of paper, torn from a spiral notebook, and affixed to the inside cover. When I'd started working here after school in the early 1980s, I'd convinced Mr. Dealey to let me add a rudimentary table of contents. Every year after that had a handwritten index numbered *1-52*, with a very brief description of the main stories that week. It was one of the first tasks that he'd turned over to me. The index for this volume was in my own adolescent hand, complete with loops and flourishes that I'd abandoned by the time I finished college.

The first week of January had been all about the weather in 1987, based on my notes. *Ice Storm. Power Outage. Wreck on Main Damages Lamppost.* I'd only vaguely remembered that storm before I opened the binder, but little tidbits began rushing back, including the bent lamppost in front of the drugstore. An elderly driver had hit a patch of ice and skidded, her car spinning round and round until the rear bumper connected with the post and knocked it off kilter.

I sneezed loudly, not once or twice, but three times. This was not the place to continue reading if I also wanted to continue breathing freely. So I carried the book upstairs, where I found Ed waiting in his usual chair in front of my desk. As glad as I was to see him, I was also a bit surprised. He usually wrote in the mornings and again for a few hours in the afternoon, seven days a week, including holidays. His second mystery,

Even in Death, was slated for publication later this summer, and he was hard at work on the third. Most afternoons, he ended up here at the conclusion of his daily walk, and I either invited him for dinner or we called Cassie to meet us at the diner.

"Have they heard back from the lab?" I asked him.

"Not yet. Billy told me they towed her car out to the impound lot late last night. Still had a few looky-loos hanging out to see it, so it's probably a good thing you talked to Tanya's mom beforehand." He frowned slightly. "There's something Billy's not telling me, though. I worked with that boy for seven years, and I can tell when he's keeping secrets."

I fought back a smile. That *boy* is in his mid-forties. "What do you think it is?" I asked.

Ed shrugged. "I don't know. And I can't really push him. He works for Blevins now, even if he's not exactly happy about it. Anyway, I figure we'll know soon enough. That's not why I'm here, though. In case you've forgotten, I promised to help you with something."

He glanced pointedly at the box with the canvases, which had now been joined by an electric drill case.

"Oh, Ed! I didn't mean you needed to rush over first thing! I haven't even been to the hardware store yet to get the stuff to hang them."

Ed grinned. "Good thing, too. Otherwise, I'd have to go to the trouble of returning all of this." He reached into his pocket and pulled out a small paper bag. "Cassie said there are four of them, right? Should be enough wire, hooks, and wall anchors here."

I put the binder down on my desk, then walked over and pressed a quick kiss to his lips. "Thank you. But you really shouldn't have made a special trip. I didn't want this to cut into your writing time."

"It's not. I'll make it up later. I didn't feel much like writing, anyway. Kept thinking about how awful that was for you and Wren yesterday. Have you talked to her?"

"Not since last night. I left her a text earlier. Told her I was here in the office if she wanted to stop in."

"Good. Anyway, I have to admit I'm a little curious to see Lucy McBride's work. She always struck me more as the type to paint with words, not on a canvas." He laughed. "I'm not sure she knew what to make out of me becoming a writer. I was kind of a late bloomer in that regard. She painted a sea of red on my papers in her class."

"You weren't the only one. Everyone said I was her favorite, and my papers still looked like a battlefield."

"Well, okay then," he said, pushing himself out of his chair. "Time for a little payback. Even if the paintings are absolutely perfect, we have to come up with at least *one* negative thing to say. For old times' sake."

"You are so bad, Ed Shelton. I am not going to speak ill of the dead. Or...at least, not of dead people I actually liked."

He clucked his tongue. "Fine," he teased. "Leave all of the hard work for me."

Someone, probably Kenneth McBride, had sealed the carton with packing tape since I'd seen it in the garage. I pried the edge loose and unwrapped the box. The first painting I pulled out was the one with the weeping willow that I'd seen the day before. I laid it flat on my desk, and Ed stared down at it with obvious interest.

"Okay, this whole saying-something-negative thing might be a little tougher than I thought," he said. "This is *good*. But...I'm going to go with the fact that she got the color of the tree wrong."

I snorted. "Don't tell me you're one of those purists who thinks every tree has to be painted green."

"Nope. I like expressionism as much as the next guy. I've got a Van Gogh print in my bedroom."

"Really?"

He grinned at the hint of skepticism in my voice. "*Maybe.* Guess you'll have to check it out one day. Is it really that hard to believe, though? You were expecting what? A black velvet painting of Elvis? Or maybe dogs playing poker?"

I blushed. "No. I didn't think that at all."

"You lie like a dog, Ruth Townsend," he said, laughing. "I'll have you know that I am a complicated man. I have many layers. *However*, in this case, our dearly departed English teacher was clearly painting a very specific tree, not simply one that sprouted from her imagination. I drove past it last week, and it was *not* blue."

I peered more closely at the canvas. "Okay, you lost me."

He pointed to the top of the painting. Off in the distance, behind the tree, was a structure—blurry but still recognizable.

"That's the old Torrance place," I said. "I haven't driven out that way since I moved back. Is it still standing?"

The Torrance House had once been a bed and breakfast, with a back deck that overlooked the river. It was upscale, and not the sort of place I'd ever been while in high school, although I knew a guy who waited tables there. And a lot of kids, Wren included, had picked up occasional jobs as servers for weddings and special events.

"The house *and* the tree are still standing," Ed said, "although I suspect both of them are nearing the end. That willow was full grown when I was a kid, and they don't usually last more than seventy years or so."

He propped the canvas, which was about four feet square, against the wall behind my desk. "And that's really the only even remotely negative thing I can come up with. You do the next one."

I narrowed my eyes at him teasingly, although I hadn't looked at the other paintings, and they might not be nearly as good as that one. Cassie had seen them, but Ed had called with the news from the river just as she'd been about to show me the rest.

When I pulled the second one out of the box, my heart leapt into my throat.

"Lover's Leap." The words were barely a croak.

Ed took the picture from me, which was probably a good thing since it was starting to give me a very bad vibe. I stepped back a few paces and sank down into my chair.

"You're right," Ed said. "Only...it's different up there now. Like I mentioned yesterday, we put a metal barrier up during my first term as sheriff. That would have been...late nineties, most likely."

The painting depicted a small gravel lot with a rope strung across the left side where the land ended and the night sky began. On the right side of the canvas, however, the rope was broken, with the loose end curled on the gravel like a dark snake. Beyond the rope, the river was tranquil and placid beneath the gaze of a full moon. Everything was illuminated by a ghostly white light.

"Okay," I told him. "I found something negative to say. This painting is creeping me out."

The bell over the door rang at that instant and, as if to prove my point, I jumped hard enough to bump my chair into the desk. It was Wren, carrying a plate of something. This didn't surprise me. When Wren is nervous or upset, she bakes. I love her way too much to ever *hope* for her to be sad or worried, but I'm practical enough to admit that her habit is something of a silver lining for her friends when she's feeling down.

"You're just in time for our art show," I said lightly.

Wren set the platter, which smelled like her cream cheese brownies, on top of one of the other desks and then joined us. She was frowning slightly, probably because she could tell that something had me on edge.

"What's up?" she asked, sitting on one of the other desks.

"Look at that." I nodded toward the canvas. "Tell me what you see."

She tilted her auburn curls to the right. "It's definitely the Freedom River. Probably somewhere—" There was a long silence, and then she looked back at me. "That's Lover's Leap. I didn't look very closely when Cassie showed it to me yesterday, mostly because I really hadn't thought about that place in years. But now that it's fresh on my mind, it's pretty obvious. And I guess I know why you looked so shaken when I walked in. It's kind of...creepy, given what we've just learned."

Even though the picture gave me the shivers, I leaned in closer to examine it. "That's where we were parked yesterday," I said, pointing to a tiny spot on the other side, far below the cliff, with its seventy-foot drop to the river below. But my eye was drawn to something else. Something in the water.

The river wasn't as calm as I had originally thought. Near the middle, a hint of green shone just below the surface right where Tanya's car had been found.

I reached out and tapped the green spot, even though I really didn't want to touch the canvas. At this point, I didn't even want to look at it anymore. "Please tell me that's not what I think it is."

Ed let out a slow whistle. "Okay. Exactly how you did you end up with these paintings?"

"The box was in Lucy McBride's garage," Wren said. "With Ruth's name on the side."

"But neither of you knew that before you went to the estate sale, right?" Ed asked.

"No," I told him. "I didn't have any reason to think she would have left me anything. The last time I spoke to her was at my parents' funeral, as she signed the guest-book. We had a nice conversation, but I still got the feeling that she considered me a disappointment for going into journalism. She asked if I was still working for *that newspaper*, in a rather dismissive tone."

Wren said, "I don't think Ruth was even planning to go to the estate sale, but I was kind of curious, so I dragged her along."

We all sat there silently for a moment, and then I pulled the last two canvases out of the box. These were both smaller, maybe half the size of the first two, and both of them looked rushed. The brush strokes were less smooth, and the effect was more of a rough sketch. You could tell they were by the same artist, and they still showed considerable skill, but they lacked the careful composition and execution of the two larger pieces.

The first one was on a black background. In the center was a misshapen dark-red circle—so dark, in fact, that the color would have been barely distinguishable against the background if not for the thin corona of light at its edge.

"Looks kind of like an eclipse," Ed said.

Wren nodded, meeting my eyes. "A *total* eclipse. And I think maybe that's supposed to be a heart. Not... like a valentine, but an actual heart."

She was right. It seemed like kind of an odd interpretation. An eclipse of the sun was something that blotted out the sun, so technically the heart should have been in the background. But that wouldn't have made a very striking image.

The final canvas looked more like a sketch than a finished painting. The focal point was a silhouette of two men against a purple backdrop. One was holding something in his hand—a stick, or maybe it was a knife?—and the other had a red logo of some sort on his back. It looked sort of like an animal's head, but it was smudged. I pressed my finger against the red splotch. It was still slightly sticky, and my finger came away with a trace of red, almost like I'd pricked myself.

I could make out the basic outline of the Torrance House and the willow tree in the background. Two other crudely drawn figures, one small and one large, were sprawled on the ground. One of the men still on his feet had his foot aimed to plant a kick near the center of the larger of the two figures on the ground.

"Wren?" Ed said. "What's the matter?"

I had been looking at the canvas, so I didn't notice her expression change. She was staring at the painting too, but with something close to horror. With a shaky hand, she pointed to the shape in the background. "That's the Torrance House, isn't it?"

"Looks like it to me," Ed told her. "Why? Does that mean something to you?"

"Yeah. It's where two guys very nearly killed my brother back in 1987."

Chapter Nine

I STARED AT WREN, mouth open. "James was in the hospital. I knew that. But...you told me he was in an accident."

"No." Wren looked down at her hands, clearly uncomfortable. "I never *told* you that. The secret wasn't mine to share, but the one thing I told Gran was that I wouldn't lie to you or Tanya."

She gave a bitter laugh. "Turned out I didn't have to worry about telling Tanya anything at all. But I left it vague when I told you. I let you *assume* it was an accident. And you were so busy trying to figure out what happened with Tanya that you didn't push."

"Wait a minute," Ed said. "I was a deputy, starting in 1984. I don't remember ever hearing about an assault over at Torrance House that year."

"Because we didn't report it," Wren said. "Gran swore it wouldn't make any difference. She was worried about retaliation. So was my dad. That's why James went to stay with Gran's sister in Chattanooga the next fall. Finished his last two years of school over there."

Wren and James had been raised by their dad, who was an Army medic. That was one reason Wren decided to enlist after high school. But the situation in Panama, where her dad was stationed, wasn't entirely stable, and he'd decided it might be a good idea for Wren and her brother to be in one location for high school. That's why they'd moved in with Gran, their dad's mom, the year Wren began ninth grade.

"I'll tell you what I remember," Wren said. "It's not breaking any promises at this point, because like I said, I told her I wouldn't lie if you asked. Anyway, as you already know, it was the same night Tanya disappeared. You and I were at that party down at Jolly's. Some July Fourth thing someone threw together last minute. Do you remember how lame it was?"

I closed my eyes and let my mind drift backward. "Yes. No one brought ice, and we had to drink hot beer. Only a handful of us showed up. We were waiting on Tanya, otherwise we'd have bailed earlier."

Wren nodded. "We were going ghost hunting or something like that. I was supposed to work that night. There was a big Fourth of July thing at Torrance House. But I didn't really need the money, since I had my enlistment bonus coming, and there weren't too many more nights that the three of us would have to spend together. So I asked the manager if James could take the shift. He didn't care, as long as he had enough bodies on hand to pass out the shrimp and chardonnay. Anyway, Tanya never showed up at the party, so we went home. I remember dropping you off and then pulling up in front of my house. It was way late, and the house was dark, which didn't surprise me. Gran never lasted much later than ten o'clock, and having worked the parties at Torrance before, I figured James just came home and fell into bed. Cell phones would have been a huge help that night. When I got inside, I saw Gran had left a note on the fridge. James was in the hospital. I left right then and drove to Maryville, only to find they'd taken him to Knoxville."

She sighed and took a deep breath. "Gran was in there with him, so it was half an hour after I got to Knoxville before I knew what happened. Someone rang the doorbell, and she found James on the porch, barely conscious. Gran took one look at him and they headed to the hospital."

"How bad were his injuries?" Ed asked.

"Broken arm. Several broken ribs, and other injuries. Some internal bleeding. They were most worried about how long he'd been unconscious, though. He said he'd blacked out totally. No drugs in his system. Some alcohol—a few of the servers had apparently finished off some of the open bottles of wine during cleanup. That earned James a lengthy lecture from Dad when we finally reached him down in Panama, but it was definitely not enough to cause him to black out. He said that tree was the last thing he remembered seeing."

Ed shook his head. "I still don't get why the hospital didn't call it in. That's assault."

"He told them he was hiking with friends. Fell. Finally managed to work his way back to the house."

"And they believed it?" I said.

She shrugged. "Probably not. But they didn't bother to question it officially."

"Someone should have called it in, Wren," Ed said. "We might have been able to track who did it. And we *would* have tried. The sheriff before me wasn't a bad guy at all."

"I know, Ed. But I wasn't the one making the decisions. And...I don't know that I'd have decided any differently if I *had* been. It wasn't the first time James had run into problems. Two guys roughed him up the first year we moved to town. James reported it to the principal, like he was supposed to. And the principal and teachers went on and on about was how it was just boys being boys. That the other boys were in the wrong, but it could have been anybody they targeted. Didn't have anything to do with the color of James's skin. But we knew that wasn't true. Gran pressed the point as far as she could without losing her job, and then...she backed off. James didn't run with a rough crowd. He never got into trouble. His GPA was almost perfect." She chuckled. "Heck of a lot better than mine. And in the end, Chattanooga was a better place for him anyway. I doubt he'd ever have gotten his scholarship if he'd stayed at a tiny school like Thistlewood."

"Did he ever remember who attacked him?" I asked.

"He said he didn't, back then. I haven't asked him about it in recent years. It's not the kind of thing that makes for pleasant conversation with his wife and kids."

Even though I was a little afraid to ask the next question, I had to know. "Did you believe him? When he said he didn't remember?"

"I don't know," she admitted. "At first I thought he was telling the truth. Over time, though? I wondered. He saw what happened with that first fight. I think it's entirely possible that he was scared. Maybe he was protecting the identity of his attackers, not for their sake but for ours."

As she spoke, a phone rang. All three of us reached for our cell phones before we realized it was the office landline.

"I thought that was just on your desk as a decoration," Ed said.

Truthfully, I was surprised, too. Most of the classified purchases, ad buys, and other business was handled online. I'd received three or four calls on the office phone since I bought the place, and two were wrong numbers.

I answered. "*Thistlewood Star*. Ruth Townsend."

There was a pause on the other end. I could hear breathing but that was all.

"Hello?"

"Ruth?" It was a man's voice, vaguely familiar. "Is this Ruth?"

"Yes." I was tempted to point out that I'd just identified myself, so of *course* this was Ruth. Instead I just asked, "Who's this?"

Another pause. I was growing impatient. "Hello?"

"It's Bud. Bud Blackburn."

I started to ask why he was calling, then I realized they must have identified Tanya's remains. I shivered, even though I'd known the news was coming eventually.

"Hi, Bud. Are you okay?"

"Can you come to the house?" His voice was deep but oddly childish.

"Sure. What's wrong?"

He sniffled, and that's when I realized that he was crying. Now the pauses on the other end made sense.

"Bud? What's going on?"

What he said next wasn't anything I'd expected.

"It's my mom, Ruth. She's dead."

☆ Chapter Ten ☆

WHEN SOMEONE CALLS and asks you to come over because a family member has passed away, you tend to assume that they dialed 911 first. But when I pulled to a stop in front of the Blackburn house, I found the driveway empty except for the old truck that had been there the previous day. Bud's, I assumed. No first responders, no sirens and lights, no curious neighbors standing on the sidewalk.

That's when it occurred to me that Mrs. Blackburn had already been taken away. Bud hadn't said *when* she died. There was no reason that he would have called me immediately. It's not like I was close to his mother. In fact, she had come quite close to telling me where to go and precisely how to get there the day before.

And now she was dead. It didn't seem possible. I had just seen her. She was upset, sure, but she'd seemed healthy enough. As I raised my hand to knock, I half expected to see her standing in the doorway again, as she had been the day before.

I knocked on the door four times. Waited and listened, but all I could hear were the birds chirping. It was a bit cooler this morning, with a few clouds in the sky, but the weather feed on the *Star's* website this morning predicted it would be hot and muggy by mid-afternoon. I knocked again and was about to give up when the lock clicked and the door creaked open. Bud looked even worse than he had the day before. His black T-shirt was inside out, he hadn't shaved, and his face was ghostly pale except for dark pockets below his eyes.

"Ruth." He seemed surprised. "You came."

"Well...you asked me to."

"I didn't think you actually would, though. Thank you. Do you want to come in?"

"Sure," I said, although that wasn't entirely truthful. It's not that I was afraid of him, but the whole thing was weird. When he called, I'd asked if it was okay to bring Wren with me. Comforting the recently bereaved is not one of my strong suits, and it is literally part of Wren's job description.

Bud had seemed nervous about that, however. He just wanted to talk to me, he'd said. So I'd agreed, but the cell phone in my pocket was on, and Ed was monitoring from his Silverado, which was parked a few blocks away.

Stepping inside, I blinked a few times to help my

eyes adjust to the darkness. The curtains had rarely been drawn when Tanya lived here. As a blue-eyed blonde, she had burned easily, but that girl had loved the sun. And even though it wasn't rational, I wanted to snatch the curtains open and let some light in. Then it might feel at least a little like Tanya's house again.

"What happened?" I asked as Bud shut the door behind us.

He shrugged. "I don't know. When I came downstairs, she was just lying on the living room floor. I checked her pulse, but she was already cold."

"What did the medics say?"

He frowned. "Medics?"

"Yes. When you called 911. What did they say?"

He shook his head back and forth quickly. "I just called you."

I glanced toward the living room. Now that my eyes had adjusted to the dimness, the room began to come into focus.

Was that a leg on the floor, extending just beyond the couch?

Yes, I believed it was.

I sighed and hurried around the couch. Mrs. Blackburn was sprawled in front of the coffee table. Her body was cold and rock hard to the touch.

"Call 911, Bud. You should've called them first!"

"Why? She's...*dead*. Even I can tell that. What good would an ambulance do?"

I stared at him. "You have to call 911. It's required." I reached into my pocket for my phone and remembered that Ed was on the other end. He wouldn't be happy that I cut the call, but I unlocked the iPhone screen and punched the three digits. For a moment, I was afraid Bud would try to stop me. That he'd rush into the room and rip the phone from my hand. But he didn't. He just stood quietly in the doorway and listened as I talked to the dispatcher.

When I finished, I went back into the foyer, not wanting to stay with Mrs. Blackburn's body any longer than I had to. Bud opened the front door, and warm sunshine poured inside.

"I can't believe she's gone," he said as he stood in the bright patch of light. "What am I going to do now?"

"You should call your aunt. And your father. I'm sure he'll want to know, even if they're divorced."

Bud turned toward me. He seemed surprised. "They're not divorced. He just got tired of living here." He looked down at his hands. "I know you never believed Tanya ran away."

"No," I admitted, "I didn't. Tanya wouldn't have done that. We were moving to Nashville in a few weeks anyway. It never made sense. Wren didn't believe it, either."

He shifted his weight, seeming uncomfortable. "I was a crappy brother. Ran around with the wrong people. But I did love her."

"Why didn't *you* speak out?" It felt wrong to ask him

that when he'd just learned that his mother, and almost certainly his sister, were dead, but I kept remembering his face that night in the hallway. "You didn't believe it, either. I could tell."

"I just had to ignore it." He scratched the stubble on his cheek. "I *had* to. That's what my parents said. And I tried. It worked for a while. Then I started drinking more, and..." He smiled sadly. "Did you know that I was married once?"

I shook my head.

"For just a few years. When I lived over in Asheville. Her name is Annie. I have a son there, too."

"That's...wonderful," I said, because I honestly couldn't think of anything else.

"I've never seen him."

"Oh." So much for me trying to cheer him up. I was failing miserably. To be perfectly fair, though, this was a truly impossible situation.

"It was my fault," Bud went on. "I couldn't stop drinking. Annie kicked me out, and I came back here to live with Mom and Dad. Her next husband wanted to adopt the baby. Didn't seem fair for him not to have a daddy there, so I said okay. I thought about leaving again, but then Dad took off, and somebody had to stay here with Mom. She had...spells."

Spells. I wasn't sure what he meant by that, but I really didn't want to ask any questions at this point. I'd never really liked his mother, but she hadn't seemed mean until after Tanya was gone. And then yesterday, she'd cranked the vicious up to eleven. Of course, I'm not sure how I'd have reacted if Cassie had been missing for thirty-two years and then someone I hadn't seen during that time turned up on my doorstep to tell me that her body had possibly been located.

"Listen, Bud, you're going to have to fill out some paperwork when they get here. I should probably go. But..." I hesitated. Telling him to call me if he needed anything was precisely why I was there. "But you can call me later if you need to talk, okay? I mean, after you talk to your dad and get everything set up with Wren—"

He shook his head. "No. She's from Maryville originally. My aunt still lives there, so that's where we'll have our services."

"Sure," I said. "I was going to say Wren or *someone*."

That wasn't true, but I definitely shouldn't have assumed anything. And they *did* have family in Maryville. "Maybe...you should call your aunt?" I suggested gently. "I mean, that's her sister, right?"

"You're right. That's a good idea."

I opened the door. "So yeah. Call your dad and your aunt. They can probably take it from there."

An ambulance pulled into the driveway. I said a silent prayer of thanks that I'd parked at the curb. Otherwise, I'd have been trapped.

And then Blevins edged his vehicle right behind my Wrangler. So much for my quick escape.

I stepped aside to let the medics enter. Bud followed

them into the living room, still giving his mom's body a wide berth.

Blevins looked up as he got out of the car, apparently noticing me for the first time. I gave him a little half wave.

"Townsend," he said, straightening his hat. "What is it with you? First Edith Morton, and now this. I'm beginning to think you magically appear every time an old lady dies. Someone looks in the mirror, says your name three times, and—poof—Ruthie's in the house."

Okay, that was *mildly* amusing, but I wasn't going to give him the satisfaction of letting him know it. "You're the one who roped me into this," I said. "Bud called me when he found her. I had no clue that it was the only call he made."

He leaned in. "Hey, I didn't mention this earlier, but Bud had a weak spot for you back in high school. If you play your cards right, you might be able trade Ed in for a younger, more agile model."

I reminded myself that he was in uniform. Punching him would probably get me tossed into a cell. So I simply uttered a few choice words that do not bear repeating and then added, "Remind me not to do you any more favors."

"You didn't do this for *me*, Townsend. I don't even think you did it out of loyalty to Tanya, although that may have been a secondary motivation. This gave you an excuse to dig around and get more details for your story. I'm guessing you didn't learn much, so I'm going to give you a scoop, so you get it straight in your little paper. The report just came back confirming what I already suspected. Tanya Blackburn was *not* the person behind the wheel of that car."

My jaw nearly hit the sidewalk. "They're certain? I mean, has there even been time for them to do a full analysis?"

"Don't need to. Tanya was what? Five-five, tops? The driver was nearly six feet. And male, which we could tell from the—"

"Shape and tilt of the pelvis?"

"I was just going to say his boots and Harley Davidson belt buckle."

"And that's why you make the big bucks, Steve. Believe it or not, there are women who are six feet tall, wear boots, and ride Harleys."

"Never seen one in Thistlewood," he said with a tight smile.

"If you suspected it wasn't Tanya, why even have me come talk to her family? Sally Blackburn is dead in there. I didn't see any sign of a struggle, so I'm guessing she had a heart attack. Maybe a stroke. An overdose, for all I know. I didn't poke around, because I wasn't looking for a story, contrary to your smug assumption. Any one of those causes of death can be linked to stress, however. So next time you *suspect* a bit of information is false, maybe you should share that with the person you con into delivering it. Mrs. Blackburn might still be alive if you'd acted like a professional."

Blevins looked a bit shaken by my comment, but he recovered quickly.

"I'll be by later to take your statement about Sally Blackburn. In the interim, maybe you should steer clear of elderly ladies. You seem to be hazardous to their health."

☆ Chapter Eleven ☆

ED PULLED into the lot behind the building just after I did. "You're grounded, young lady. Our agreement was that you would leave the phone on so that I'd know you were safe." He gave me a wry grin. "And yes, I know why you cut the call. If you'd waited on Bud Blackburn to take the initiative, I'm guessing he'd still be trying to decide whether to use the phone downstairs or the one upstairs to call 911."

"Blevins just told me the body wasn't Tanya. It's male."

"Oh," he said, looking as confused as I felt.

"Get this, though. He says he suspected it wasn't Tanya even *before* it was confirmed, based on boots and a belt buckle. And yet he asked me to go tell Tanya's mom —and Bud—that it was *probably* Tanya. He knew I'd do it, too. All he had to do was mention the possibility that they'd find out through the grapevine, and I trotted off to do his bidding."

I planted a hard kick into one of my Jeep's tires.

"Feel better?" Ed asked, as he thumb-typed a text, most likely to Billy, into his phone.

"No. I still want to kill him, and now my foot hurts. And it doesn't make sense. That car was Tanya's baby. We even joked about how she wouldn't let *anyone* drive it. Not Bud, not me, not Wren. She said it was an ugly hunk of junk, but it was *her* ugly hunk of junk."

"Could be some guy she was seeing. There are plenty of guys who have to be the one behind the wheel."

It was possible, but I wasn't buying it. Tanya's taste in guys ran more toward what Cassie sometimes called *emo*. Artistic types. The only one she'd been seriously interested in had graduated and headed off to art school two years before we graduated. I started to protest that Wren and I would have known if she was seeing someone, but it felt like I was rehashing all of the arguments I'd made to any adult who would listen in the weeks after Tanya vanished.

So I just shrugged. "More likely someone stole her car. Guys in boots and Harley belt buckles were *not* Tanya's style. Either way, I'm not sure it changes anything. I can't really think of a scenario where someone crashed Tanya's car into the river and she's alive."

We went in through the back door to find Wren flip-

ping through the 1987 binder I'd left on the desk. Cassie
had pulled up a chair next to her and was munching on
one of the brownies, which were indeed the kind with
that yummy streak of cream cheese in the center.

"What are you doing here?" I asked Cassie. It was
still only a little after ten, and she's not a morning person,
so I was a little surprised to see her out and about.

"I've been working," she said with a little grin. "I just
came over here to get some paper so that I could sketch
out some ideas for setting up the shop, and I found Wren
here with brownies. They're good, too. Is Tanya's mom
really dead?"

I nodded. "If I had to guess, I'd say it happened late
last night."

Ed continued texting while I gave them a brief overview of my past half hour. Then he stashed the phone in
his pocket. "Any clues as to how she died? Signs of
struggle or..."

"No sign of struggle at all. She was just slumped onto
the carpet, cold as ice. And...I'm a lousy reporter. I
should have at least poked around in the kitchen and
bathroom. Checked to see if there were pill containers.
Or something. I was just so flabbergasted that Bud hadn't
even called 911."

"How's Bud doing?" Wren asked.

"He's holding it together, but it's a bit like he's...um...
well, like his elevator doesn't go to the top floor these
days."

She and Ed both nodded, then Ed said, "That's pretty much any day ending in *y*. I don't know how sharp Bud Blackburn was in school—he was probably in first grade when I graduated—but I dealt with him several times as sheriff. Good-tempered fellow, wouldn't hurt a fly, but he gets falling-down drunk in public every few months. I had an agreement with Jay over at Beatty's to cut him off when he started getting sloppy, and give us a call. The officer on duty would come around to the bar and drive him home rather than letting him walk. It's all of five blocks, but driving him home meant the school-kids and tourists wouldn't have to see good old Bud passed out on the sidewalk the next morning. But Blevins decided that a thimbleful of gasoline and ten minutes of a deputy's time, when he was probably just cruising around anyway, was a waste of county funds. Started booking Bud for public drunkenness, which did no one an ounce of good. For all his talk of hating paperwork, Steve Blevins is happy to generate another pile if it means he can make a few people miserable."

Although Ed's comments were pretty much in line with what Wren thought of Blevins, she seemed a bit surprised. I think it was hearing that many words coming from Ed in one serving. He doesn't usually rant, but I'd already heard him go off on several occasions about the changes—few of them good—that had occurred in the sheriff's department since Blevins took over.

"Well, Steve had just rolled up when I left, so Bud

will have to deal with that glorious ray of sunshine in addition to making arrangements for his mom. I told him to call his dad or his aunt, because I'm not really sure he can handle it on his own."

Cassie pulled in a deep breath, almost like she was steeling herself against something, and then asked, "So, Wren...how long before they bring the body to you at Memory Grove?"

The question surprised me a bit. During the whole Edith Morton case, my daughter had admitted that she *sees things* on occasion. Ghosts, I guess you'd call them. In the past, Cassie had tended to steer clear of all things death and funeral related after being pretty shaken up at my parents' funeral when she was a teenager. While I wasn't entirely surprised by her revelation, I haven't pushed for details, since she doesn't really seem to want to talk about it. The one thing she did tell me was she was trying to get past her fear and accept the ability as a gift. Maybe even a useful one.

Cassie still wouldn't go to Wren's house, though. Wren lives above the funeral home, and I think that's a bridge too far for Cassie. The fact that she was even asking Wren a question about the whole business of death and burial was a big enough step.

"Oh, they won't be bringing Mrs. Blackburn to my place," Wren told her. "Probably Heavenly Rest over in Maryville, but definitely not Memory Grove."

While I already knew from my discussion with Bud

that she was right, it still seemed a little odd to me that Wren said this with such complete certainty. I didn't want to press the point with the others around, however, so I made a mental note to ask later why she was so sure that Sally Blackburn's body would be taken elsewhere.

"Did you handle the arrangements for Lucy McBride?" Cassie asked.

"I did," Wren said. "That wasn't too long after your mom moved back here. It was a packed service. Ms. McBride taught for nearly fifty years, so she'd interacted with pretty much everyone who lives in Woodward County."

Cassie looked over at the canvases. "Did anyone mention that she painted?"

Wren shook her head and looked to me for confirmation.

"I don't remember anything about her having any hobbies other than reading," I said. "Maybe it was something she took up recently. The biggest question for me, though, is why she picked *these* subjects."

Ed shrugged. "Speaking both as a cop and as a writer, the answer in cases like these is usually the obvious one. The person who painted those pictures had something to do with the crime. And maybe she had a guilty conscience. The only problem with that is that I can't even begin to imagine Ms. McBride killing anyone."

"But she clearly knew something," Wren said as she gave Ed a brownie. I declined...they looked good, but checking Sally Blackburn for a pulse I knew I wouldn't find seemed to have killed my appetite.

"Her house was right across from the Blackburns," Cassie noted. "Do you think maybe she saw something? Or heard something?"

"Maybe," I said, but it didn't really feel right to me. Along with my parents and Mr. Dealey, Lucy McBride was one of the adults I'd tried my best to convince that there was something odd about Tanya disappearing.

"And that might explain Tanya," Wren said. "But three of those paintings seem connected more to what happened to James. I hadn't really thought a lot about them happening on the same night. I mean, Tanya didn't show up at the party, but we didn't really have a clear sense that she was missing for several days. Looking at those paintings, I'm starting to wonder if the two things aren't connected somehow."

"Your gran worked at the school," I said. "Was she friends with Ms. McBride?"

Wren made a seesaw motion. "Friendly, but not friends. Which leaves James..."

"Do you think he might have confided in Ms. McBride?" Ed asked.

"No," Wren said. "I mean, he liked her well enough, but I don't think she's someone he'd have sought out. He was in the same grade as Kenneth, but they weren't really close either. And we didn't even mention what happened within the family. Gran said we were to *let it go*. Pretend it never happened. The one time my dad alluded to it, when the three of us were driving down for James's wedding back in 2009, she gave him the side-eye and turned up the radio. End of discussion."

"Do you think James would be willing to talk about it now?" I asked her.

"Maybe. But I have a dentist appointment in half an hour. How about I call you when I get back? Oh, and take those brownies home with you. I made extra."

Ed's phone signaled an incoming text as Wren was leaving. He typed something back and then looked up at me. "Blevins left out one little detail. The body in the driver's seat wasn't Tanya Blackburn. She was the one in the trunk."

I just stared at him for several seconds. "So, that's new information, right? Results that just came in from the lab that Blevins didn't know about yet?"

"You must be a psychic, Ruth. That's the very question I just texted to Billy." Ed's phone buzzed again. "And the answer is...*no*. They don't have any results from the lab, but the body was female. Plus, Tanya's purse was in the trunk, and the driver's license was still legible."

I frowned. "But why? Not why she was in the trunk, although I definitely want to know that, too. Why would Blevins just tell me about the driver?"

Ed raised his eyebrows. "That's an easy one—at least for anybody who's worked with the guy. We were deputies together for nearly a decade, and he was always looking for a way to one-up me. He was the world champion at trying to take credit for things I'd done. When I ran for sheriff, I kept him on for the first couple of years and saw him pull the same stunt with Billy. That wasn't the reason I let him go, but let's just say it was one of many things that factored into the decision. Right now, Steve Blevins is scared that you're going to make him look stupid again, just like he did when the whole Edith Morton story broke. He's planning to sit on this for a few days until you've published a print version with a story that's not entirely wrong, but far from complete. Then he does his big reveal, with a press conference if he can get one of the reporters interested."

"And yet he was so very worried yesterday about how this would affect the tourist season," I said wryly.

"He probably *is* a little concerned about that," Ed admitted. "But the car has been in the river thirty-two years. It's not like we've got a killer roaming the streets of Thistlewood. And even if we did, I doubt it would outweigh the fact that he has an election coming up next year. Blevins will go for the free publicity. And..." He grimaced. "You're probably not gonna like this part, but I really need you to find another source for the information I just gave you about the body in the trunk."

"Why?" Cassie asked.

I had started to ask the same question, but then it hit me. "Billy needs cover."

Ed nodded. "He's got a wife and two kids, and I'd hate to put his job at risk. I'm not sure Blevins would actually fire him, to be honest, since he shoves the lion's share of his job onto Billy's shoulders. But you never know."

I sighed. "Are they using the TBI Lab in Knoxville?"

"Yeah, but I doubt you'll be able get anything out of them."

He was probably right, unfortunately. The Tennessee Bureau of Investigation has forensic labs in Knoxville, Memphis, and Nashville. I'd actually had two regular sources at the Nashville lab when I was a reporter with the *News-Journal*, one of the largest papers in the state, and they might have still talked to me if the body was there. But without previous contacts at the Knoxville lab, it would probably be hard to find anyone who would give me the time of day, especially now that my business card bore the logo of the *Thistlewood Star*, with a circulation that barely edged into triple digits.

"Well, I guess I'll be sticking with the vague version currently on the website until I can find a second source. And I'm not likely to find it hanging out in the office."

"Speaking of hanging..." He nodded toward the paintings still propped up against the wall. "What's the verdict? Are these still going up?"

"Eww," Cassie said.

I had to agree. "No. They go back into the box. But first, I'm going to take some pictures of them. And then I'm going to hunt down Kenneth McBride, because I have a few questions I'm really hoping he can answer."

"You do know you're going to have to tell Blevins, right?" Ed said. "This is...evidence."

I grimaced. He was right, though.

"Can we hold off at least until I talk to Wren's brother?" I asked him. "This involves him, too. And Wren."

He shrugged. "Tanya's disappearance has been unsolved for thirty-two years. And to be honest, I doubt he'll know what to make of it anyway. So, yeah...I don't see what holding off for a few hours will hurt."

Chapter Twelve

"DO you think he's still in town?" Cassie asked as we turned onto Poplar Avenue. "You said before that he seemed like he was in a hurry to get back to California."

At the estate sale, Kenneth McBride *had* seemed in a hurry to get everything wrapped up. I was fairly certain that he'd spent at least most of his childhood in Thistlewood, since Lucy McBride had been teaching when Ed was in school, and he'd graduated almost ten years before I had. Kenneth might even have been born in Woodward County, since Ms. McBride had some family in the area. So he'd probably have been considered *from-here* by the town natives back then. But thinking back to his expression as he'd stood in the living room, selling his mother's belongings, I realized that you could lose that designation over time. Yesterday, he had seemed very much like an outsider.

"I suspect that he *is* ready to get back home. But when Wren went back to pick up the books she'd bought, he told her that he'd timed things so that he could handle the estate sale and the closing on the house in the same trip."

And sure enough, a generic-looking car that was almost certainly a rental was parked in the driveway. We got out of the Jeep and rang the bell. Music was playing inside, something classical and dramatic. Beethoven, maybe. I rang again, and the music cut off. Kenneth opened the door and looked from me to Cassie.

"Good afternoon," he said, looking a little puzzled.

I fought the urge to check my watch. Was it afternoon already?

"You're the girl who bought those paintings," he said to Cassie.

I extended my hand. "I'm Ruth Townsend. We actually went to school together, although I was a few years ahead of you. I spoke to you briefly after your mother's service."

He nodded. "I thought you looked familiar. I saw a lot of people that day. Yesterday, too. You were friends with Bud and Tanya across the street, right?"

I said yes, even though it was probably stretching things to say that Bud and I were friends.

"If you're wanting to return the paintings," he said, "I'll give you your money back and you can just donate them to Goodwill. I'm trying to clear everything out, not bring things back in. How much did you pay?"

I shook my head. "No. It's nothing like that."

Cassie grinned at him. "And you shouldn't be offering me money back. You gave them to me."

He laughed softly, and I realized it was the first time I'd seen him smile. "Thanks for being honest. Everything has been a blur the past few days, and I'm still on California time. My brain doesn't kick in until around one. Is there something I can help you with?"

"I hope so," I told him. "I had a couple of questions about the paintings."

He moved out of the doorway. "Come on in. I'm not sure that I can be much help, though. I don't even remember what they looked like. Well," he added, nodding toward Cassie, "except for that one you showed me with the blue tree."

We followed him into the house, which was now stripped almost entirely bare. Everything was gone except for a card table and a chair in the dining room. Four large boxes with DONATION scrawled across the front were stacked in the corner.

"I'm still trying to figure out where that box even came from." His voice echoed in the bare room. "I didn't think there was anything in the garage aside from the holiday decorations. Mom really didn't have a lot of artwork. As you probably could tell, she decorated with books. There were a few pictures of me as a kid upstairs, but..."

"She never hung any of her own artwork?" Cassie asked. "That seems odd."

I shrugged. "I don't know. A lot of artists are like that. It's a shame, though. They're really good."

"Wait...what do you mean, *her* artwork? You don't think Mom painted those, do you? She couldn't even draw stick people."

"But...she signed them," Cassie said.

I pulled out my phone and opened the photo of the one with the blue willow. Then I zoomed in on the lower right-hand corner. "See? L. McBride."

"Okay, I was already confused about where these came from, but now I know something is wrong. Someone is playing a joke on you. Mom never painted anything. She didn't even paint these walls. I took care of it because she was already having trouble using her hands, even when I was in high school. You knew she had arthritis, right?"

I shook my head, but then I remembered the oversized pen she'd used to sign the guestbook at my parents' funeral. "Was it severe?"

"It wasn't *too* bad until she was in her sixties. But the last few years of her life, she could barely even hold a book. She got an e-reader, and that made it a little easier. And audiobooks. Otherwise, she'd have gone crazy." He sighed and his features softened. "I'm sorry, Ruth. Mom didn't paint those pictures. I don't know who did but it wasn't her. It's just not possible. But...why is it so important? I mean, they seemed pretty good, but..."

"Did you hear about the car they pulled out of the river yesterday?" Cassie asked.

"Um...no. I've been kind of busy."

"It was Tanya Blackburn's Mercury," I said, opening the painting of Lover's Leap. "That green splotch is right where they found the car. She disappeared—"

"Fourth of July," he said. "1987. Yeah. I remember. Bud and I weren't really close or anything. But he'd come over and we'd shoot hoops sometimes. They had a trampoline in their backyard when we were in elementary school, and I'd go over to jump sometimes with him and Tanya. Anyway, I didn't see him much after that summer. Always got the sense that he was angry at Tanya for skipping town and leaving him here. Which I get. I didn't exactly stick around after graduation, either. But...you're saying Tanya didn't go to Nashville?"

"She was in the—" Cassie began, but I gently cut her off.

"We *think* she was in the car they pulled out of the river yesterday. The lab hasn't issued a report yet. And we believe the other three paintings are connected to another incident that happened that same night. Do you remember James Lawson?"

"James? Sure. Kind of hard to forget the only black kid in my class. Wicked smart. He was only here two years, though. Moved to...Knoxville, maybe?"

"Chattanooga," I said. "He's an attorney in Virginia Beach now."

I showed Kenneth the images of the paintings on my phone.

"Torrance House. Yeah. We went there for my graduation dinner."

"Did you remember hearing any talk that summer about a kid getting beaten up over there? The evening of the Fourth?" I showed him the rough painting of the three guys in front of the willow.

Kenneth gave me a pained look as he took my phone for a better look. "I don't, but...that's not saying anything. It's been thirty years, Ruth. Between work and three kids, some days I'm lucky if I remember what I had for breakfast." He glanced back down at the image on the phone and tilted his head, then shook it again. "The only thing that jumps out at me is that jacket. Or rather, the logo."

"Did you know someone who wore one like it?"

"Not personally," he said. "But it looks like the River Rats. A regional biker group. Most of them were in their early twenties. Stomped around in leather jackets and boots. Back when we were little, every kid in Thistlewood—well, almost all of the boys and at least some of the girls, too—would meet down in the park on holiday weekends to watch them roll through. One of them had a grandma who ran a campground just outside of Thistlewood, so he was here a lot during the summer. I don't remember his name, but Bud might know. They hung out sometimes. He was too young to be an actual member, but he said they let him ride along sometimes. Don't know if that helps, but..."

I glanced at Cassie. "Yeah, I think it actually might."

We thanked him, said goodbye, and headed back to the Jeep.

"We're going to the Blackburns' house, right?" Cassie asked, looking a little confused. "It's just two blocks away."

"Yes," I said, "but I don't want Kenneth wondering why I left my vehicle in his driveway. And you're going to be staying in the car anyway. Bud's kind of skittish."

"Um...it sounds like he was also part of a biker gang at one point, Mom. Maybe you should let the cops talk to him? Or wait until Ed is here?"

"Ed Shelton can't follow me around all the time while I do my job, Cassie. I interviewed many, many people when I worked at the *News-Journal*. You never expected me to wait for an armed guard then."

She frowned. "By the time I was old enough to really comprehend that fact, you were at the editor's desk. I'd also never had anyone point a gun at me, like we did a few months back. That kind of changes your perspective."

"Fine, I'll take you home first," I told her.

"No, you won't."

I sighed. "We're already here, okay? I just want to ask him a couple of questions. And yes, Bud's a little weird. But he loved his sister. He's not going to hurt me."

As it turned out, the entire discussion was a moot point. Bud's truck wasn't in the driveway. I knocked anyway, just to be sure, but no one answered.

"Good," Cassie said when I got back into the Jeep.

"Because next time you can bring Ed. Otherwise, I'm going to worry about you. And I know you don't want that because you're a good mother who would never cause her daughter distress."

"Hey, wait a minute," I said. "Did we just swap roles, like in *Freaky Friday*? Because I'm pretty sure the mom is the one who is supposed to lay down that sort of guilt trip."

Even though I made a joke out of it, her point hit home. She had been through a traumatic experience. So had I, but for a much shorter time, and I'd had a few close calls when working in Nashville. Maybe taking a few extra safety precautions wasn't a bad idea. It's not like she was saying I needed to bring Blevins along.

We turned into the parking lot behind the building, and I huffed in annoyance. It was almost as if thinking the man's name had conjured him up. Or his car, at any rate. This was a shared lot, so it was possible that he was bothering someone else.

"I'm heading over to the shop," Cassie said. "Dean and I may grab dinner afterward, so don't plan anything for me. *And don't go back to see Bud without Ed. Capisce?*"

"*Capisce.*" I wasn't going to argue with her about it right this minute. She needed to get to work, and so did I. *Capisce* simply meant that I understood, not that I agreed. Later, we were going to need to have a long talk, not just about any leftover issues she might have from her brief abduction, but also about my job and boundaries. I'd spent over a decade as an investigative reporter, usually without a partner. Yes, ten years at an editorial desk had probably dulled my instincts a bit, but those instincts were still there. They just needed a bit of sharpening.

The bigger issue for me was that I wasn't willing to give up my autonomy again. Cassie's father had treated me as an equal at the beginning of our relationship, otherwise there wouldn't have *been* a relationship. But after Cassie was born, his attitudes seemed to shift. He clearly felt that the day-to-day responsibilities of parenthood were mostly the woman's job. Joe began to act as though his career, his priorities, were more important than mine. I'm not sure that I'd even have accepted the editorial position if it hadn't been for the fact that someone needed to have a steady schedule. I couldn't be off chasing clues about a murder or bank robbery, because someone needed to be there with Cassie in the evening, and Joe simply wasn't reliable on that count. Tanya's parents had left an indelible mark on me—I would not be that kind of mother, even if Joe was turning out to be that kind of father.

And so I'd pushed aside the part of my career that I'd found most satisfying, because I loved Cassie more.

I still did.

But Cassie was a grown woman now, and it felt like I was falling back into a familiar pattern. If Ed and Cassie

—or even Wren—would be worried, I couldn't go alone. Ed had insisted on listening in when I went to talk to Bud Blackburn today, and I had agreed, even though my instincts told me that Bud was not a danger. I should have told Ed firmly but politely that I'd be fine. That I'd see him back at the office after my conversation with Bud was finished.

Long story short: my entire world had been upended when Joe Tate decided he'd rather be single. That was partly my own fault, because I'd gradually handed over bits and pieces of myself—my career and my autonomy. I would never let that happen again. Ed and I were clearly moving toward a closer relationship, and with Cassie here now, we were almost forming a family unit. I liked it. In fact, I loved it.

But I didn't want to lose myself again. I wasn't willing to have my job restricted by whether a man— even a really good one like Ed—was available for backup. I had my pepper spray. I'd taken self-defense classes. And more importantly, I had my instincts, which were getting sharper by the day. They had served me well for many years, and with any luck, they'd serve me well for many more.

Which meant I needed to schedule a serious conversation with two of the most important people in my life. Come to think of it, with all three, since Wren had chimed in to support Ed today when he insisted that I keep the phone call open so he could listen in.

Wren had known me the longest and had been my

sounding board for most of the key decisions in my life. She had been all about me taking back control of my life during the divorce and move to Thistlewood. So I'd test out my Declaration of Independence on her. If it went over like a lead balloon, that would give me time to make adjustments before talking to Cassie and Ed.

Chapter Thirteen

I UNLOCKED the back door and stepped into the press room. Stella, my ancient printing press, and Blanche, the slightly younger Linotype machine, stared at me woefully, reminding me that they were still waiting for me to find either the time to figure out how to make Stella's repairs myself or else fork over the exorbitant sum to have the one expert in the country who still worked on dinosaurs like her fly here to get it back into order.

Blanche was still working fine, but it didn't really help to have the typesetting capacity if I couldn't print the paper in-house. I'm pretty sure the workers at the company in Knoxville that currently cranks out my print edition each week would be rolling on the floor laughing if I carted in eight giant printing formes instead of submitting my copy online.

My one attempt at DIY had failed miserably. After waiting several months for the replacement part to arrive,

I carefully read the Heidelberg manual I'd found online, watched a few online videos from a printing museum, then rolled up my sleeves and got to work. Halfway through, the spring grew tired of my amateur efforts and sprang for the nearest exit—which happened to be into the belly of the beast itself.

I still haven't found it. I'd swept out dozens of pens and paper clips and more peanut M&Ms (Mr. Dealey's addiction) than I could count, along with a red star-shaped earring. Mine were red, Tanya's were blue, and Wren's were white, and we'd bought them from one of the booths at the annual celebration in Thistlewood Park, the very last time the three of us were together.

We'd spread a blanket out on the lawn and watched the fireworks, with the smells of hot dogs, funnel cakes, and the ever-present mosquito spray filling the air. The thing that made me a little crazy was that I couldn't remember anything we'd talked about or done, aside from buying the earrings. We'd probably joked about guys we were crushing on or talked about our upcoming exit from Thistlewood. It was just another conversation, one of many we'd had, and one of the many more that we all assumed we'd have.

When the last smoky plumes of the finale faded away, we'd split up. Tanya had only managed to get an hour off for the fireworks, and she had to be back at the diner to help with closing. Then she'd meet us at Jolly's for the second round of fireworks—the illegal, decidedly less-professional variety that would sound off along the river from midnight until two or three in the morning, or whenever a deputy arrived to tell us someone had complained. The official story was that we were spending the night at Tanya's house, which meant curfew was nonexistent. But then she never showed at the party.

Was there a pair of blue star-shaped earrings in the trunk of that Mercury? I was pretty sure that was the case. Blevins would never confirm it, but maybe Billy would at some point. It wasn't that I needed confirmation that the body was hers. Obviously the lab report would confirm that. But it would give me a sense of whether she wound up in that trunk on the night of July 4th or at some later time.

I glanced over at the rows of font cases that lined the walls, knowing I'd need to go through Mr. Dealey's list to find an original font for Tanya's obituary. I already had an idea, but it would require a little online detective work to figure out what font was used on the cover of the last Bonnie Tyler album she owned. And I'd need to come up with one for her mother's, too, although I didn't plan to expend a lot of effort on that one, given how little effort she'd expended on finding her daughter. Like Mr. Dealey, I'd print every obituary in a font we hadn't used elsewhere, even if I hadn't particularly liked the person. But it would be something fairly standard—like Century Gothic, Palatino, or Arial.

My thermos of coffee was still in the front office. I decided to grab it and one of Wren's brownies before diving in, since I'd sort of skipped lunch. It was a good thing I did, because someone was at the front door.

Not Blevins, as I'd feared, but the younger of the two brothers who'd found Tanya's car. He was about to walk away, since the sign was flipped to CLOSED. I waved both hands, one of which was now holding a brownie, to catch his attention and then hurried to the front to let him in.

"Sorry," I told him. "I was in the back and forgot to flip the sign."

"I'm Jack," he said. "We spoke yesterday outside the diner?"

"I remember. Please come in. Would you like a brownie?"

He shook his head. "I'm sorry about yesterday. Rich can be obnoxious, especially when he's upset. And even though he didn't want to admit it yesterday, he was upset. He took off for the surface as fast as I did when he saw that, even though he tries to act all cool now."

"That's pretty typical," I said. "People process things differently."

"I don't think he processes things at all. But I'm not here to talk about Rich."

"Does he know you're here?"

Jack snorted. "He does not. But he's met some girl who came to the reunion with Zoe, our cousin. Told him I was going drive in to get something from the diner. As long as I bring them back pie, I'm covered." He glanced down at the floor. "You said you knew the victim?"

"I knew one of them."

"There was more than one?"

At least the comments on the website had relieved me of the need to avoid speculating on the information that Billy gave to Ed. "Rumor has it there was a body in the trunk," I told Jack. "I'm pretty sure that's the girl I knew since the car belonged to her. The guy you saw, the one behind the wheel—the police still don't have an identification on him. Or if they do, no one has told me yet."

"Do they know why your friend was in the trunk?" he asked.

"No. Her name was Tanya Blackburn. She just... disappeared without a trace more than thirty years ago. Everyone thought she ran off to Nashville. She was going to be a singer. I never believed it, but I'll admit there was a tiny part of me that hoped I was wrong and she was still alive somewhere."

"Sorry," he said.

I shrugged. "There's also a part of me that's glad to have closure, to be honest. To know that I hadn't been wrong about our friendship."

"So what did you want to know?"

That was a good question, and I wasn't quite sure how to answer. I had felt there was something I could learn from talking to the brothers back at the diner. I still felt that way as we sat there, even though I couldn't really put my finger on it. That had often been the case when I interviewed people, though. It was an instinct, a sense that even if you weren't sure why you were digging, there was *something* under the surface.

"I just want to know what you saw," I said. "In your own words."

"Okay." He sighed, and his shoulders seemed to sink inward. "We got some new snorkel equipment for Christmas. We wanted to practice diving under so that we could see more, and that area is kind of still." He took a breath. "Rich is bad about wanting to get up early. We had gotten into town late the night before, and the thing I remember most about that morning is how much I was dragging. He practically had to put me in the truck. I tried to get him to go alone and leave me back at the cabin."

He looked at me. "But that's dangerous, so I went anyway. We hadn't been at it long. Maybe twenty minutes when I first saw the car. The river is deeper out there in the middle than you would think, and at first, I had no idea what I was looking at. It looked like a hunk of mud, or a huge boulder of some sort."

I nodded but didn't say anything, and he stared beyond me to the paintings propped up on my desk. "That's—um. Isn't that the spot where we found the car?"

"Yes. It's something a friend of mine gave me. I was just...looking at it as I started writing the story. To kind of set the scene."

I felt bad because that was mostly a lie, but I wasn't sure what else I could tell him that would make sense.

"Anyway," he said after a moment, "the sun was shining down, and there was this one perfect ray...I'll never forget it. It shot through the water like a sword, and everything around me just kinda shimmered. It was beautiful...until it wasn't anymore. There was a glint of metal, and I realized I was looking at a car. I decided to dive down for a better look. Didn't even think about the possibility that there might be someone in it. Rich followed me, which was a little surprising. As you probably noticed, he likes to play the boss because he's older. But truth is, I'm the better swimmer. And he's probably regretting following my lead. I'm pretty sure that sight followed him into his dreams just like it did mine, even though he'll never admit it."

"I worked for the *Nashville News-Journal* for years," I told him. "And I saw quite a few things that followed me into dreams. It will be rough for a bit, but it fades." *Most of the time*, I thought, but I decided not to add that. There were definitely a few sights that still made the occasional cameo in my dreamscape, but those were usually connected to cases that were never solved.

He glanced down at my hand, still holding the brownie. I was having second thoughts about eating it given the topic of discussion, but apparently he was having second thoughts about refusing my offer. Maybe talking about it was helping. Or maybe it was just that teenagers are bottomless pits, and it takes more than a skeleton in a submerged car to kill their appetites. So I motioned to the plate behind him again, and this time he grabbed one.

My phone signaled a call from Ed. "I need to take this," I told Jack. "There are some bottles of water under the desk over there if you want something to wash down the brownie."

I stepped into the back room. "What's up?"

"I can't just call to hear your voice?"

I laughed. "You *can*, but you don't. Not in the middle of a writing session."

"Busted," he said. "Just wanted to give you a heads-up that Bud has apparently taken off. I don't know if he's got something to hide or if Blevins just scared the living daylights out of him, but Billy tells me they're putting out an APB. His mom had a whole bunch of prescription meds in her system. Mixing Vicodin and Valium is a bad idea, especially if you wash them down with vodka. No clue whether it was accident, suicide, or foul play, but running off doesn't look good."

"No," I said. "It doesn't. I don't think he killed her, though. Why would he have called me to come over?"

"No clue."

"Listen, I've got one of the two snorkelers out in the front office. He just dropped by..."

Ed laughed. "Out of the blue."

"Okay, no. Like I told you before, I saw them at the diner and asked if they'd talk to me. But I didn't try to track them down. The younger one just showed up. So... let's both get back to work."

"Yes, ma'am, right away, ma'am."

I cut the call and then went back into the front office.

"Sorry about that. Where were we? And you can definitely have another brownie if you want. They'll probably go stale otherwise."

That was a total lie. Cassie, Ed, and I would polish off every single one of those babies. But we didn't really need all of them, so I was glad when he grabbed a second one.

Okay, *kind of* glad.

"I was telling you about finding the car," Jack said. "The weirdest thing, though, was that we hadn't really planned on going to that spot. Everyone else was swimming down at the location near the campground, on the other side of the marina, and we could have practiced with the snorkels over there just as easily. Rich and I had to hike down to this place, a good fifteen minutes. But we had an entire day to kill, since most of the adults had gone over to the casino. My cousins are..." He rolled his eyes. "Let's just say we don't have much in common. And the night before, over at the marina snack bar, some guy had told all of us this dumb local legend about a bootlegger who buried one of those old army chests down there, full of money, rather than turn it over to the government."

"I never heard that *particular* legend," I told him, smiling. "The one I heard was that there was a trunk of Confederate gold that they didn't want to turn over to the Yankees. I think old people make those things up just to give kids something to do."

He laughed. "Yeah. The man who told us was pretty old and really into it. Even drew us a map. My cousins just blew him off. I mean, Rich and I didn't believe him for a second...the river's not that deep, even in that section. If there was actually treasure, someone would have found it, especially if he had a map. I even asked the guy why he didn't go look for it himself if he had a map. He got that look...the one people get when you catch them in a lie. And he actually had to think about it for a good two seconds before coming up with the excuse that he couldn't swim. But to be fair, I think he'd been drinking."

"Could you describe the guy? The one who gave you the map?"

He thought for a moment. "Like I said, kind of old. Maybe sixty? And he'd been drinking. His eyes were all bloodshot, and he smelled like stale laundry. Which probably should have been our cue not to trust him."

I stopped to think for a moment. The man he'd described was almost certainly Bud. It would have been fairly obvious even if I hadn't suspected that he was the artist behind my newly acquired paintings.

"And...you told all of this to the sheriff yesterday?"

Jack nodded. "Most of it, yeah. Maybe not *all* of the details. You ask more questions than he did."

A prickle of unease crept along my arms and back. "Do you still have the map?"

"No. Rich gave it to the sheriff."

As if on cue, Steve Blevins strolled through the front door. I hadn't flipped the sign, so it still said *Closed*, but in retrospect, I should have locked the darn thing since I knew there was a two-legged skunk in the vicinity.

"Pretty sure I told you not to bother these guys, Townsend." Blevins glanced down at Jack's hand. "And here I find you luring kids in with gingerbread, like that witch in *Hansel and Gretel*."

"It's a brownie," Jack said. "And she didn't lure me in. I looked up the local paper online last night to see if there was any more information about the car. Saw a pretty cool story from a few months back about a murder case. Since you never called to give us an update, I decided to see if she had any details."

"Su-u-u-re," Blevins drawled. "But maybe you should get back down to the campground and keep out of trouble, hmm? I have to take her statement about an entirely different crime scene."

Jack hesitated for a moment, then got up. "Thanks, Ms. Townsend. It was nice talking to you. And again, I'm sorry about your friend."

☆ Chapter Fourteen ☆

I *REALLY WISHED* Jack hadn't said the last bit, because I was pretty sure that Blevins wouldn't be happy that I'd mentioned Tanya. But my mind was still back on the last two words the sheriff had spoken: *crime scene*. Last I'd heard, Mrs. Blackburn's death was precisely that—a death. No hint of foul play. There was a decent chance that Blevins was just blowing smoke, but now I wondered if something might have changed.

But Blevins was looking past me, exactly as Jack had done a few minutes ago.

"That's Lover's Leap. Where did you get those?"

"At the estate sale. Like I told you before."

He crossed over to the desk, grabbing a brownie without even asking. Then he crouched down to examine the canvas more closely. "Lucy McBride painted this?"

"I don't know," I told him. "Her name is at the

bottom, but her son seems to think it was forged. She had arthritis. And no, I don't know why anyone would forge her signature onto a painting. You just called Mrs. Blackburn's death a *crime scene*. Why?"

He didn't answer, just kept staring at the painting. "Did you buy this before or after we pulled up the car?"

"Before," I said, although I couldn't see what difference it made.

"Seems kind of a weird coincidence, doesn't it? And you didn't think this was something I should know?"

"And you didn't seem to think I should know Tanya's body was stuffed in the trunk," I said, glaring at him. The words were out before I even thought about Ed's caution that I needed to find another source, but it was too late to pull them back now. "And before you tell me you're under no obligation to share information with the press, I was under no obligation to deliver that news to Mrs. Blackburn yesterday."

"How did you know that?" he asked.

I floundered for a moment and then remembered that I *did* have another source for that information. Not a solid one, but it would have to do. "I didn't know it until you confirmed it just now. But hold on a sec and I'll show you." I turned my chair around to face my computer.

Once I had the *Star Online* loaded, I clicked the button to turn on comments and pushed the laptop toward Blevins.

"I turned the comments off last night so that we wouldn't get any more speculation," I said. "But face it,

Steve, you can't keep a secret in Thistlewood. Not unless you plan to close down the diner and confiscate cellphones and computers. And still, everyone would probably gather in the park, like blackbirds on a telephone wire, to dish about the latest. It's just human nature."

"These comments are ridiculous," he said. "An ice-cream truck? You're telling me this is how you knew—"

"All of them are ridiculous except one. Tanya's car. Tanya's missing. Tanya wasn't the body in the driver's seat. Logical deduction."

I'm not sure if he believed me, but he shoved the computer back and picked up one of the other paintings. I watched his face for a moment and could almost see the hamster wheel running inside his head.

"I think you could be on to something here, Townsend. Maybe Lucy McBride killed this guy. Tanya, too."

It was all I could do not to laugh. I didn't think for a single moment that Blevins believed that. For one thing, she'd been his English teacher, too. The idea of frail, bookish Lucy McBride murdering anyone was laughable.

What I didn't know was whether he'd managed to connect Bud Blackburn to the description of the man the boys had seen at Jolly's Marina. Or even if they'd given him a description, since Jack said his questioning hadn't been especially thorough.

I was about to repeat my question about why he'd used the words *crime scene* when Blevins asked. "What are these others? That looks like the old Torrance place. And that's a knife, isn't it?"

"Maybe. Do you think that's Mrs. McBride holding it? Or maybe she's the one kicking the person on the ground?"

Blevins gave me an annoyed look. "It's two men—" He stopped, realizing that I was mocking him. "Funny."

"I don't know what they're supposed to be, Steve. They were all together in a single lot. I wanted the one with the tree."

Blevins pulled a set of wire-rimmed reading glasses from his front shirt pocket and picked up the Lover's Leap painting. I had no idea he wore glasses. Too bad they didn't make him look any smarter.

My phone buzzed with a text. It was from Wren, saying that she was back from the dentist and I should just let myself in and meet her back in the storeroom.

Blevins was still hunched over the canvas, clearly interested in the spot in the river. "That's definitely supposed to be the car, sinking into the river after plum-meting from here." He tapped the cliff, where the broken guard rope lay like an undisturbed snake.

"Which is what you think actually happened, isn't it?"

"Yes," he said absently. I almost had the sense he'd forgotten that he was talking to me. "Given how the car was positioned at the bottom of the river, I really don't see how it could've been any other way. The current isn't strong enough to turn a vehicle like that. Not today, anyway. I have no idea what it was like in 1987."

He propped the painting back against the wall, then took out his phone and snapped pictures of all four. "Don't get rid of them," he said as he started for the door. "And don't mention them to anyone else. Or in the paper. I'm not going to confiscate them...at least not yet."

I found that I really didn't care. After the last twenty-four hours, I would've gladly delivered them to the station myself.

"Thought you had questions to ask me," I said. "About the other *crime scene?*"

Blevins hesitated for a moment. "I'll come back later."

"Make it tomorrow," I told him. "I have plans."

He looked like he wanted to argue, but he just slammed the door behind him and headed off around the building.

I waited until I saw his car drive past on Main Street, then left for the short walk to Wren's house. It was nice to get outside and stretch my legs a bit. Maybe the fresh air would clear my head so that I could begin to make sense of what I'd learned in the past few hours.

The man Jack and his brother spoke to at the marina had to have been Bud Blackburn. Tanya's car was undoubtedly the buried treasure he'd been hoping they'd find, mostly likely with a big fat X marking the spot. But why? Why tell a bunch of kids to search in an area, knowing they would find the bodies, especially if he'd had anything to do with it?

Furthermore, I was all but certain that he was the painter, and those works practically screamed guilty conscience. I didn't know if he'd been planning all along to get the painting to me, or if I'd just been a target of opportunity. It was entirely possible that he'd seen me pull up across from his house on our way to the estate sale. He might not have recognized me after all these years—no one looks the same at fifty as they did at seventeen. But he'd have recognized Wren, and even if he's a fry or two short of a Happy Meal these days, Bud could have put two and two together. When I was there to tell him and his mother that they'd found Tanya's body, he'd said that he'd heard I was back in town.

I couldn't believe he'd had anything to do with killing Tanya. Every instinct screamed out at me that this wasn't true. It was pretty much inescapable, however, that he knew who killed her. He probably knew who was responsible for beating Wren's brother, too.

Bud was leaving all of these clues, almost like a trail of breadcrumbs. It was the only answer that made sense. But he'd had me there at the house today. He'd called me when his mom died. If he had something to tell me, why not just tell me then? Or call me? Why leave vague clues that I might not find and might never piece together even if I did?

It didn't make sense.

And yes, there was a part of me that could see him

killing his mother if he lashed out in anger. To be brutally honest, I could see a *lot* of people lashing out at Sally Blackburn in anger, maybe even being tempted to throttle her if she got up in their face and yelled like she had at me the day before. If there had been signs of a struggle, I'd have been more willing to entertain the possibility that Bud had killed her.

But could I really imagine Bud going online, researching the lethal combination dose of whatever drugs might happen to be in the family medicine cabinet, and then persuading or forcing his mother to take them?

No. I really could not.

So, if he didn't kill her, why run?

The only answer I could come up with was that Bud was afraid of Blevins. Afraid that even though he hadn't killed his mom, the police might think he had.

Or maybe Blevins had pieced together that it was Bud at the marina, and those were the questions that now had him on the run.

Either way, Bud Blackburn clearly wanted me to figure out what happened to Tanya. Maybe the problem before was that I hadn't asked him directly if he *knew* anything. I'd simply asked him why he didn't speak out and say he didn't believe she'd run away. Wren, my very best friend, had been keeping a secret all these years because the secret wasn't hers to tell. Because she'd made a promise, and Wren was the type of person who always kept a promise.

Maybe Bud was, too.

☆ Chapter Fifteen ☆

"HOLD ON," Wren said, looking at me as if I had grown a second head. "You think *Bud* painted those pictures?"

"Yes."

"Because you saw paint on his hands and shirt?"

Wren put the dust-cloth down on top of the casket she'd been polishing. That's one of the tasks with her job that I hadn't even considered. There were eight different models arranged near the middle of the room, like new cars on a dealer's lot, and I guess they collected dust just like anything else. The room also had a couch with a coffee table that held a large catalog of other caskets, complete with specifics, features, and options. I'd sat on that couch next to her after my parents' accident. Making decisions I didn't want to make. Aside from the embalming room down in the basement, where I had been precisely once, this was my least favorite place in Wren's house.

"Ruth? Are you with me?"

"Sorry." I turned my attention back to her. "That's not the only reason. That was just one clue of several."

She gathered her cleaning supplies and then nodded toward the door. "Okay, then. Let's head upstairs. I'll put on some tea and you can begin walking me through."

I readily agreed, eager to get upstairs. The upper floor of this place is far more warm and inviting, without the emotional baggage this area holds for me.

"I really don't like this," Wren said as we headed upstairs. "If you're right, and Bud did paint those pictures, that means he knew what happened to his sister. And he didn't say anything."

I grimaced. "I know."

"And that means he knows something about what happened to James, too. Might even have been involved in what happened."

She had a point.

While the tea brewed, we sat at the table in her cheery kitchen, and I laid out the evidence for her to consider, including the new information about Mrs. Blackburn and Bud's abrupt departure.

"I just don't see why he'd plan to leave those paintings at the estate sale," Wren said. "Why not just drop them off at your office? Or your house. You weren't even planning to go. It's not like there was an RSVP list he could have checked or anything."

"True," I said, "but I don't think that part was really planned. I think it was more a target of opportunity. Bud was planning to get the paintings to me at some point. I thought I saw someone at the upstairs window that day. There were so many people that it would have been really easy for him to leave the box with the canvases in the garage. Someone might have thought it a little odd that a guy was carrying something back into the sale instead of out, but they probably thought he just changed his mind, you know? And another reason I think he acted on impulse was because he wasn't quite finished with that last painting. It's smudged in places from him shoving it into the box too soon, and the red splotch on that one guy's back was still kind of tacky even this morning." I held up my index finger, which still had a tiny spot of red in the center. "Maybe he applied that last touch when he saw us parking across the street and shoved it into the box."

"And I guess leaving your name on the box was a bit of insurance," Wren said. "No one else would take it, and if we hadn't seen it, there would have been a good chance that Kenneth McBride would have called you to say you'd forgotten it and needed to pick it up. But here's what bugs me about all of this—if Bud knew something, why not just *tell* you?"

I gave her a sad smile but didn't say anything.

It took a moment, but eventually she followed my point. "You think he's protecting someone?"

"Maybe. Or maybe he made a promise and this is his way of getting around it. He still hasn't *told* me anything. Not a single word. If he leaves pictures and I manage to piece the clues together, he hasn't broken his promise. It's a loophole, just like the one where you told Gran that you wouldn't lie to me or Tanya if we asked you outright."

Wren sighed and pulled the tea bag from her cup. "I'm sorry about that. It's still a lie of omission."

I squeezed her hand. "Like you said, the secret wasn't yours to tell. Maybe if I'd asked him directly, but I can't do that now. And speaking of secrets, do you really think James will be willing to talk about that night?"

She nodded. "I sent him a text while I was waiting at the dentist. This isn't the sort of thing I'd feel comfortable simply springing on him, especially since Annie or the kids could be around. I explained everything, and he's expecting us." Her head tilted to the side. "What's the matter?"

For a moment, I hesitated. Wren probably wasn't going to like what I was about to say, but she would be there when I talked to James, and it was a question I'd almost certainly have to ask him.

"Do you think he knew about Tanya, Wren? Not that I think he had anything to do with it," I added quickly. "Not at all. But the paintings seem to suggest that the two events are somehow connected, and..."

"No," Wren said. "I don't think he knew. James understood how much not knowing hurt both of us. If he'd had any clues, or anything that could have given us closure, he'd have told me. And I'd have told you, no matter what promises I gave to Gran. But I know you have to ask."

I nodded. "Wish we didn't have to do this by phone," I said. "It would almost be worth the drive to Virginia Beach—"

Wren laughed and went over to the small desk in the corner of her dining room. "You just want to go to the beach, girl. Not that I blame you. It's been a crappy couple of days. But we have the next best thing." She held up her iPad. "FaceTime. So you can still get all of those visual cues to help you decide what to ask next."

She propped the iPad on the coffee table in front of us. I looked at myself in the little top square as we connected to Virginia Beach, over five hundred miles away. The little thumbnail that showed my reflection was horrifying, and I wished I'd had time to do something with my hair. I hadn't seen Wren's brother in at least twenty years. Technically speaking, this was a professional interview with a source, and I didn't really look all that professional after the long day I'd had.

Several seconds of musical beeping passed, and I was beginning to wonder if he was there. Then James Lawson answered. He looked almost exactly as he had the last time I had seen him, when Wren was on leave and I'd met her for a weekend at Virginia Beach. The years had been kind to James. With the exception of a touch of gray here and there in his goatee, he still could've passed for mid-thirties.

His face lit up when he saw Wren. "Little sis," he

yelled, although Wren was older than him by two years. She was, however, technically *littler* than him, and had been since he was around fourteen. "It's good to see you."

He glanced at me on the screen and squinted. "And Ruth Townsend. I haven't seen you in forever."

"It's good to see you again, James." And it was, even though I was a little worried about the topic we'd be broaching.

"I heard you moved back to Thistlewood. You're as crazy as my sister, you know that? I hope y'all are staying out of trouble?"

"Why would we do that?" Wren said. "Trouble is where the fun is. We seek it out, believe me."

He chuckled. "I don't need to believe you. I've seen it in person."

"How's the beach today?" Wren asked.

"Crowded, I suspect," he said and then stared at the camera. "I don't go out there on a holiday weekend any more than you go to the river. Although...I guess the two of you *did* end up going to the river this weekend." His expression suddenly turned serious. "I was sorry to hear about Tanya, Ruth. I know how close the three of you were. So, fire away, Ruth. Not sure how much help I can be, but..."

"Did Wren tell you about the paintings?" I asked.

"She told me that there *were* paintings but didn't really go into detail. They're by Lucy McBride, right?"

"I'm now thinking probably *not*. But we'll get to that

in a minute. Let me show them to you. This would probably be easier if I emailed them, come to think of it.
You're not going to be able to see much detail from me
holding my phone up to Wren's iPad."

So I forwarded the pictures to Wren, who forwarded
them to James. It took a couple of minutes, and in the
interim, he told me about his kids, who hadn't even been
born the last time I talked to him, although Wren had
certainly shown me plenty of pictures. And I told him
Cassie, who he'd actually met on the trip to Virginia
Beach, was doing well.

When the pictures came in, James was silent for
several minutes while he looked at them. I could tell
when he got to the one of the fight in front of Torrance
House because he sucked in a deep breath.

I sat there with Wren, and we awkwardly drank our
tea, waiting for him to finish. Finally, he turned back to
the camera and said, "How did Lucy McBride know
about this? Wren...you didn't..."

"No," Wren said. "I kept my promise. Gran would
have had my head. Ruth is my witness on that point. I
never even told her until today, and that's only because I
had the wind knocked clean out of me when I saw that
painting. I'm as much in the dark here as you are. But...
Ruth has been digging in a bit deeper. She doesn't think
Ms. McBride painted them."

"So who do you think painted them? Kenneth?"

Wren and I glanced at each other. That thought

hadn't even occurred to me. Apparently not to her either, judging from her expression.

"Do you...do you think Kenneth could have been one of the guys who attacked you?"

James's eyes widened, and then he laughed. Not just a chuckle, but a full belly laugh. When he finished, he said, "Do you even remember Kenneth back then? If he'd punched someone, it would have been like getting slapped with a wet noodle. That guy couldn't even climb the rope in gym class."

He had a point. Kenneth was still kind of thin, but back then, he'd been scrawny. And bookish like his mom, but leaning more toward comics and science fiction, much to her chagrin. She'd been almost as biased against "genre fiction" as she was against my career in journalism.

"So yeah, no way was Kenny one of the guys who jumped me. He was actually one of the few people I hung out with a bit in that town. My point was more that he might have heard about it. Bud lived on that same street."

My stomach sank. "You think Bud was one of the guys in that picture?"

James nodded. "I think that's very likely. He worked that same party. My only question is whether Bud was one of the guys on his feet or the one on the ground there next to me. Bud could be an okay guy, when he was on his own. He had...aspirations, though. Wanted to be part of that rat club."

"River Rats?" I asked.

"You got it. I never saw it that night, or if I did, I don't remember. But that red smudge on the back of the guy's jacket...the one not holding the knife? That *could* be one of them. The last thing I remember was that tree and then a noise behind me."

"Could you start at the beginning," I said, "and just tell me what you remember about that night?"

"Sure. I worked the shift for Wren. Thought she'd been real sweet to give me the chance to make some cash when I went in, but I kind of understood why she'd been willing to give it up by the time the night was over. That manager kept us hopping the entire time, and I realized why Wren had come home the few times she worked one of those events at Torrance looking like she'd been wrung dry. That huge back deck area had been rented out by someone—a company maybe, or maybe just a bunch of rich friends—because it has a good view of the fireworks. There were maybe twenty of us, total, and we walked around with hors d'oeuvres and trays with wineglasses, which I really wasn't supposed to be handling at sixteen, but it was a private party, so I guess they were pretty lax. When the party ended, he took volunteers for cleanup crew. It was an extra hour's pay, so I said sure. Supposed to dump out the rest of the wine, but it was all sort of wink-wink. The manager knew we sneaked out the back and chugged it. I got stuck with mopping down the floor when we were done. So I was the last one heading out."

"What time was that?" I asked.

He shrugged. "Fireworks ended at nine. I think the party ended at ten. Maybe another forty-five minutes for cleanup. The manager offered to give me a ride when he locked up, but I still hadn't decided whether I was turning left at the end of the drive to go to the party at Jolly's or right to go home, so I told him I'd just walk. By the time I reached the willow at the end of that long driveway, my feet had made the decision for me. I was already bone-tired, and it was nearly a mile back to Gran's house, and no guarantee I'd be able to get a ride back from the party if Wren wasn't there. Last thing I remember seeing was that tree, like I told Gran when I got back to the house. Something whacked me hard upside the head. Guess they dumped me on the porch, because I don't remember how I got there."

"When did Bud leave?" I asked.

"Not sure. He didn't stick around for cleanup, so probably around ten. Maybe ten fifteen. Wren said he's still there in town, though. Why not ask him?"

"Bud Blackburn is missing," Wren said. "The sheriff seems to think he killed his mother. Ruth isn't convinced on that point, but she thinks he could be behind the paintings."

"If he'd just snapped and killed her, I might believe it. But...I don't think he's capable of engineering her overdose. Do you think it was Bud that attacked you?"

"To be honest, I never suspected Bud. When I was bullied at school, he never really joined in. He was on the periphery sometimes, but not one of the ringleaders."

"Probably because he knew Tanya would kick his butt," Wren said.

"Could be. The problem with Bud was more that he wasn't willing to take a stand that might make someone not like him. Even if that someone was a jerk. Maybe *especially* if that someone was a jerk. He was always a follower, not a leader. If his friend in the Rats jacket started throwing punches at me that night, I can't guarantee he didn't join in, but I'm almost certain he wouldn't have had the guts to stop him."

"His friend?"

"I can't remember his name. Had just gotten himself bounced out of the military, though. Seemed kind of proud of it, which gives you a hint about his intelligence. He was older than Bud, obviously. Twenty, maybe? Not from Thistlewood, but spent most summers here. His grandmother ran a campground a few miles out of town—"

"Kenneth mentioned him when Cassie and I stopped by to ask about the paintings. Do you know his name?"

"No. One reason I said I thought Bud might be that second lump on the ground, though, was that he said he and this guy had a bit of a falling out. They'd been at the diner earlier that day, and whatever the guy said to Tanya, it made Bud mad. Although, like I said, Bud didn't really make waves, so this guy—" He stopped. "*Frank*. His name was Frank. I don't know the last name. That might even have *been* his last name. But anyway,

Bud was probably just talking big. Probably never even told Frank he was mad at him."

"So, you think this Frank guy was in love with Tanya?" Wren asked.

James laughed and shook his head. "Oh, no. There was nothing romantic about it. He definitely thought she was hot, though."

I turned to Wren. "Can you remember anything Tanya said that night at the park?"

"Not really," she said. "Buying those earrings. Her needing to get back to the diner, and that she'd see us later. Maybe...maybe Patsy might remember something?"

She looked hesitant to even suggest that, and I understood precisely why. Yes, Patsy might remember something. But asking Patsy questions about it would probably result in at least one other person finding out. I didn't know if she and Jesse Yarnell had progressed to the point of actual pillow talk yet, but I had my suspicions. And if Jesse Yarnell got hold of a secret, you might as well buy a billboard and plaster it in giant letters, because the entire town would know by the end of the day.

"Maybe if you explained why we need to keep it quiet?" Wren said.

"But that's really all I can remember," James said. "What they didn't beat out of me, time has taken away. I'm sorry."

I squared my shoulders. "It's okay. You've definitely given me something to go on."

And he had.

Like James, I wasn't sure whether Bud was one of the figures fighting or one of the two on the ground. But I was certain that he'd been there that night, and certain that it was somehow linked to Tanya's disappearance. To Tanya's *death*.

Looking at the images Bud had painted, it occurred to me that he'd also given me a pretty clear idea of something else—where he was hiding.

☆ Chapter Sixteen ☆

IT WAS after five by the time I left Wren's place. I'd sent Ed a text and asked him to meet me in Thistlewood Park after his walk instead of at the office. It was a nice evening, and I was kind of hoping that being there, in the very same park, might trigger some memories about my last conversation with Tanya. The place was almost as crowded as it had been that Fourth of July. The diner was packed, so a lot of people had opted to grab a bite from one of the food trucks in the square. Experts say that the sense of smell is the one most likely to trigger memories, so I looked around to see if there was a funnel cake truck. Nope. Just tacos, hot dogs, and barbecue.

No memories were surfacing, but the food trucks had definitely triggered hunger. My entire consumption for the day had been a brownie, a cup of tea, and several quarts of coffee. So I wandered over to the barbecue truck and ordered two pulled pork sandwiches, with coleslaw and their jalapeño mac and cheese on the side. The girl working the truck was a friend of Ed's niece. She asked if I wanted to go ahead and add banana pudding for Ed, because this wasn't our first picnic in the park, and she knew he'd eventually come over to order one if I didn't.

"Sure," I told her. "Actually, make it two. And two bottles of water."

Once I paid for our dinner, I made my way back to the fountain in the center of the park. My stomach rumbled, but I told it to hush. We could wait until Ed got here. And since I could see his familiar figure about a block away, coming down the sidewalk toward me, my stomach didn't press the point, although I was pretty sure it wasn't going to allow me to nibble at my sandwich like a lady once we were finally allowed to dig in.

Hunger aside, I had two ulterior motives for plying Ed with food. First, I hoped he'd be able to call in a favor to find information on Frank, last name (or possibly, first name) unspecified, whose grandmother ran a campground back in the 1980s and who had a most-likely dishonorable discharge from the military. Second, I needed to let him know that I was going out looking for Bud Blackburn tonight. That I was going alone, but I would call him if something came up.

Ed waved when he spotted me and headed for the wooden bench where I was waiting. Those benches, which are positioned around the perimeter of the fountain, have been here as long as I can remember. The wooden planks are weathered by years of sun, rain, and snow, and scarred by the countless etchings of teenagers over the years. *Avril was here 07. Bev and Trey 4-eva. Thistlewood Thunderbirds Rule.*

"Dinner is served," I said as Ed approached, nodding to the bag on the bench. He gave me a quick kiss and then peeked inside.

"If I ever doubted that you are a keeper," he said, "which I haven't by the way, this would settle the matter. You even bought me two banana puddings." He grinned, because he knew from past experience that even though I love it, I rarely have room for more than a few bites.

"Dream on, mister. I never got around to lunch."

"How did your visit with the good sheriff go?" Ed asked as he unwrapped his sandwich.

"About as you'd expect, although we never actually got around to talking about Mrs. Blackburn. He came in just as I was finishing talking to the boy who found Tanya."

"Ouch," he said. "Bet he was tickled pink to find you talking to one of his witnesses. What did the kid say?"

He had to wait for the answer, because I was already digging into my mac and cheese. Between bites, I filled him in on my afternoon—the conversation Cassie and I had with Kenneth, Jack's revelation about the man they'd seen at the marina and the treasure map, and the discussion Wren and I had with James.

"You have had a busy couple of hours," he said.

"Oh, and that's not all," I told him. "I should have

stashed those paintings back in the box, because Blevins saw them when he came in. That's actually why he never got around to asking me about Mrs. Blackburn. He recognized Lover's Leap and even spotted the car beneath the river."

"You're kidding!" Ed said. "That may actually be a first. Blevins is about as observant as a blind cat. Did he ask about the other paintings?"

"He asked about the one with the guys fighting, but I told him I didn't have a clue. Which wasn't *entirely* true then, and is even less true now. Do you think there's any chance you can search for information on the guy that Kenneth and James mentioned? This Frank guy."

"Don't need to search," Ed said. "Pretty sure they're talking about Frank Daniels. Grandmother was Nellie Daniels. Ran the Tip Top Campground about a mile past the turnoff for Jolly's Marina."

"Is she still alive?" I asked.

"Nope. Campground was closed for a while after she died. Reopened a few years back, but I don't think it's anyone kin to her. The only kin she had that ever came around Thistlewood was Frankie, and he was a real piece of work."

"You knew him?"

"Arrested him once. Threatened to on several other occasions when he came through with that biker group from up in Knoxville—"

"The River Rats," I said. "Patsy mentioned a biker group was in town this weekend. Is it the same one?"

Ed nodded. "Same group. They come down this way most holiday weekends. Might even have some of the same members, but they're old, and fat, and not nearly as much trouble these days."

"Is Frank Daniels—" I began, but stopped because Ed was shaking his head.

"I haven't seen Frankie in..." There was a long pause, and I could tell that he was trying to figure out exactly *when* he'd last seen him. "Probably the summer of 1987."

"Okay," I said, taking a long, slow chug from my bottle of water while that information sank in. "So...he's the body in the car."

"I think that's a pretty safe bet, and I'm feeling kind of dense for not putting that together earlier, when you mentioned the belt buckle. Not that it was really distinctive. All those guys wear that kind of stuff. And Frankie was just one of the many lowlife rabble-rousers I dealt with as a law enforcement officer. The last time I thought of him was probably when his grandma died back around 2000. Someone—probably Blevins, thinking back—said he was an ingrate. Stayed with his grandma all those summers and didn't even show up for her funeral. I told him that the guy was most likely in prison, which he had to admit was immensely possible. And that's the last time Frank Daniels even crossed my mind. You think Tanya was seeing him?"

"Nope." I repeated what James had told me about the incident at the diner. "I'm going to have to see if

Patsy remembers anything. Highly unlikely after this long, but..."

Ed looked at me for a moment over the top of his pudding. "You still don't believe Bud killed anyone, do you?"

"No, I don't. At the very least, I don't think he killed Tanya. Why would he leave these clues if he did it?"

He shrugged. "Sometimes people have a guilty conscience. Sometimes they want to get caught. The theory that Blevins—and yeah, Billy, too—are going on is that his mom knew, but she didn't turn him in. And then when the car was found, he made her a killer cocktail."

I shook my head. "Not buying it. And exactly how does Frank Daniels fit into that theory? Why was Tanya in the trunk? And what about James Lawson? There's something else going on, Ed."

We sat there for a few minutes, finishing our dinner as we watched the water shooting like a small geyser from the center of the fountain. I could tell that Ed didn't entirely agree with me. He was going for the most obvious answer, and to be fair, I didn't blame him. Even though we didn't have all of the pieces, Bud was the most logical suspect.

"Let's talk about something happy," I said. "Okay?"

"Sure." He smiled. "What do you want to talk about?"

"How's the book going?"

He grimaced. "I thought you said you wanted to talk about something happy."

"When do I get to read it?" I asked.

"You know the deal."

"Yes, yes. As soon as it's finished."

He leaned in and gave me a kiss. "You'll be the first. I promise. And I was actually teasing you. I'm almost done, which is a minor miracle considering everything that's been going on. And I still have an entire day left before my deadline, so I might even make it."

I stared at him. "A day? Your deadline is—"

"Tomorrow."

"Why didn't you tell me? I wouldn't have been bothering you all day. Heck, I'd have delivered your dinner."

"You're not bothering me. Anyway, I needed to see you to test out the dedication. I'm thinking: *To Ruth—the sleuth who stole my heart.*"

I laughed.

"What's wrong?" he asked, still grinning. "Too corny?"

"Maybe. But I love it anyway. And now, you need to *go home.* Do not even think about calling me until you've emailed that manuscript. I mean it."

He gave me a fake pout. "Yes, ma'am. As long as you promise to stay out of trouble."

"I actually can't promise that."

"I'm serious, Ruth. I know you've been wondering about Tanya for all these years, and you really want to know exactly what happened. I get it. I've had cases that just ate at me until they were solved. But there's nothing urgent here. Give me until tomorrow...and maybe a little of the next day to catch up on my sleep. Then we'll figure all of this out."

I held his gaze for a long moment and then said, "You may change your mind about the dedication by the time I finish, but...we need to talk. This is my *job*, Ed. It's the same job I did in Nashville. I investigated drug dealers. Quite a few murderers, too. In most cases, I didn't work with a partner. My pepper spray is in my purse. I will have a phone with me, the new one that doesn't constantly lose a charge, and I have a panic button app connected to your number. If I need backup, or if I even think it's possible that I *might* need backup, I *will* press the button. I really don't want to worry you or Cassie, and I don't want either of you angry at me, but I'm going to go out looking for Bud tonight. If anyone else is there, I'm not sure he'll talk. I owe it to Tanya to find out what happened, and you know Blevins. If he can make the case stick, he will. Even if Bud didn't really do it. And last but not least...*it's my job.*"

Ed was silent for a very long time at the end of my little speech. Then he gave a slow, rueful laugh. "Well, I guess the shoe is firmly on the other foot now, isn't it?"

I didn't have to ask what he meant. Ed and I had shared divorce stories not long after we met. His marriage hadn't lasted nearly as long as mine, and they'd parted amicably, even though it wasn't really what he wanted. He'd married Lori when they were both in their mid-twenties, not too long after he became a deputy. She worried every time he walked out the door. Became stressed every time she heard sirens. Even bought a police scanner so that she'd know anything that happened when he was on duty.

About four years into the marriage, he'd come home to an empty house and a note. Lori said she wouldn't ask him to choose between her and his work, because she didn't want him to be unhappy. But she'd realized she just wasn't cut out to be a policeman's wife. He'd tracked her down and offered to quit, to find some other line of work. And he said he would have, even though they both knew he'd have been miserable. She told him no and moved down near Atlanta, where her sister lived. A few years later, she'd married a guy who managed a K-Mart, They had a couple of kids. She and Ed still exchanged letters at Christmastime, and Lori sent him a sweet note of congratulations when he published his first book. She's pretty and seems really nice. And yes, I am a little bit jealous.

"I'm sorry," I said.

"No," he told me. "I'm the one who should apologize. You're not helpless, and you've got a darn good head on your shoulders. I'll help anytime you ask me to, but I need to stop acting like a caveman."

I grinned and opened my banana pudding. "You weren't acting like a caveman."

"Yeah, well, you can't read my mind. Because the whole time you were making your case, I wanted to fling you over my shoulder and carry you home so you'd be safe. Wrap you in bubble wrap. But I also want you to be happy, so... fine. Go do your job. Trust your instincts. Just make sure you call me when you get in. Because I *am* going to worry."

"I'm sorry."

"Don't be," he said. "Comes with the territory when you lose your heart to a sleuth. But...a bit of advice from someone who knows Blevins?"

"Sure," I said. "I'm always happy to take insider advice."

"It's poker night. Back before my accident, we all played together. Afterward, we sort of had an unspoken agreement that Blevins would go one Sunday and I would go the next. Kind of like the divorced couple you can't invite to the same party. Anyway, it's his week. Billy will be there, too. Even the new deputy will likely stop in to play a hand or two. Personally, if I was planning to rob a bank or...you know, go in search of a guy who may or may not have murdered his mom, I'd do it between nine and midnight."

"Very good advice, Mr. Shelton. In case I, you know, need to rob a bank tonight while you're finishing your book." I looked down at my dessert. While I could have finished it, I'd probably have regretted it, so I swapped my mostly full cup for his now-empty one. "And that very good advice earns you a second banana pudding."

Chapter Seventeen

AFTER ED WENT HOME, I walked down to the diner. It was as crowded as I'd known it would be, but I didn't need to place an order. I just needed to talk to Patsy. And one thing I knew from many years as a customer was that Patsy doesn't miss her smoke break. Every two hours, give or take ten minutes, she walks out the kitchen door that leads to the parking lot and the dumpster beyond, and lights up. So I just leaned against the wall and waited.

At 7:04, the door opened. Patsy jumped like a scared rabbit. She cursed loudly, then laughed as she lit her cigarette. "Are you trying to give me a heart attack, Ruth Townsend?"

"I'm sorry. I just need to ask you something, and—"

"It's true, ain't it? That was Tanya's car they pulled out of the river."

I nodded. "That's kind of what I needed to ask you

about. She worked that last night, the Fourth of July, before she disappeared. I know you thought she'd gone to Nashville, and I don't blame you for thinking that. Lord knows she talked about it enough. But now we know that she didn't, and someone told me that there might have been an...altercation of some sort that day. Between Tanya and one of those bikers. Maybe her brother, too."

She sighed and then took a long draw from the cigarette before responding. "It's been thirty years, Ruth. More even. We had *altercations,* as you called it, all the time. Did you ever wait tables when you were in Nashville?"

"No. Worked fast food, but I didn't wait tables."

"Well, any girl who has knows that you're going to get your bottom pinched or have some fool catcalling you at some point. Now that it's my place, I kick 'em out if they give one of my girls trouble. But Daddy was from a different era, and he was still running the diner back then. He'd always tell us to ignore it if we could, but if they got too bad, he said to dump a pitcher of ice water in their lap to cool them off. Happened at least once a week in the summer. Oopsie." She grinned. "The bikers were always bad about that kind of stuff, but I don't remember anything in particular that day."

"How did the bikers treat your black customers?" I asked.

Patsy looked a little surprised. "There weren't any issues that I recall. Daddy wouldn't have tolerated any of that. To be fair, though, you know how Thistlewood is.

We didn't get a lot of minorities in here even during tourist season back then. Mostly just Wren and..." She paused, taking another puff before she went on. "Funny. I wouldn't have remembered this to save my life if you hadn't asked, but Wren's brother was in that day. Same time as the River Rats. Joseph, I think his name was?"

"James. He's an attorney in Virginia Beach now. Was there trouble?"

"Not with him. At least, not exactly. I just remembered him coming in to place a to-go order around noon for him and his grandma. Tanya rang him up. They were laughing about something, and then James left. Tanya went over to refill the sodas for the bikers' table...I think maybe Bud was with them, too. And I don't know what was said, but she accidentally-on-purpose poured a pitcher of tea on one of the guys. Not her brother, but one of the others. Oopsie."

"What did he do?" I asked.

"Nothin'. He knew better. We'd called the cops on them a few years before. He knew we'd do it again. He just stomped out the side door with his britches lookin' like he hadn't made it to the bathroom on time."

"But...you said nothing unusual happened that day. I mean, when I asked you back then."

She took another puff and laughed. "Because nothing unusual *did* happen. Like I said, couple of times a week we'd have to cool some guy off. Why are you asking about this now? Do you think that guy had something to do with Tanya driving her car off—"

"Tanya didn't drive off the edge, okay? You can tell Jesse and anyone else to just cut that rumor right now."

"Then what did happen?" she asked.

"I don't know yet. But I'm going to find out. And when I do, everyone can read the actual truth—not a bunch of speculation—on the front page of the *Star*. Thanks, though, Patsy. You've been a big help."

When I arrived back at the house, Cassie was already there, curled up on the couch with a book and Cronkite, who completely ignored my arrival. I know precisely where I stand in this cat's hierarchy. Cassie is number one. I'm number two, although he's willing to ignore me quite often if Ed or Wren stop by. I stopped being insulted by this long ago, deciding to simply believe that Cronkite is so secure in my affection for him that he feels free to suck up to other people who are physically capable, and possibly willing, to open a few cans of Fancy Feast.

Cassie held up a finger, which meant she was about to finish the page, and I watched as her eyes scanned over the last few lines of print. She smiled at something she'd read, marked her place, and closed the book.

"How was your night?" I asked her.

"Good," she said. "We grabbed an early dinner at that Mountain View place you mentioned. They were packed, though. We had to eat in the bar."

"That doesn't surprise me. Lots of tourists in town this weekend."

She nodded. "Yep. Everyone was talking about the car found in the river."

I sighed. "I suspect that'll be all anyone talks about for a long time. Especially when word gets out that there were two bodies in the car and not just one."

"Have you heard anything else about Mrs. Blackburn?" Cassie asked.

"It was apparently an overdose. Or rather, a fatal combination of prescription medications and alcohol. And Bud Blackburn is Blevins's top suspect, for both his mom and Tanya. Especially now that he's disappeared."

"What do you think?" Her eyes searched my face.

"It's the obvious answer. I just don't think it's the right one. But...I'm willing to enlist you as a second opinion once I pour myself a glass of wine. You want one?"

"Sure."

I opened a bottle of merlot and pulled two glasses from the cabinet. A movement from the yard caught my eye as I was filling them. "Cassie! Take a look." I nodded toward the sliding glass door. I'd bought a curtain after our last ordeal, but we rarely closed it. Cronkite hated the thing, and the sight of the woods behind the house always made my day brighter.

Cassie slipped her book, *The Woman in Cabin 10*, onto the coffee table. "Is someone out there?" she asked warily.

"Sort of. It's Remy. Out by the shed."

Cassie went to the window and peered out at the yearling bear placidly wandering around our backyard. "Listen," she said, "I know he probably saved our lives and all that, but I've got to be honest. Remy kind of scares me."

"It's just Remy," I said, even though he scared me a little bit, too. "He wouldn't hurt us."

I wasn't sure why I felt so defensive toward the bear on my lawn. Cassie *was* right. He was a wild animal.

"I'm not saying he would," she replied. "Just that I'm not sure that he *wouldn't*, either."

I ignored her. "What are you doing out there, buddy? Are you okay?" Great, now I was talking to a large woodland creature through my sliding glass door as if he could hear me. As if he could understand me. The strange thing about the bear in my backyard is I've always thought he *did* understand me. Almost like he was someone I used to know who came back in animal form to watch over my house from the dark woods. My furry guardian angel.

Remy rolled onto his back.

"Aw, look at him," I said.

Cassie carried the wineglasses over to the table. "Um, that's...cute, I guess?"

There was a part of me that wanted to go out and rub his belly, although I decided it might be best not to admit that to Cassie. Not that I'd ever actually do it. I didn't even pet him when he was tiny and I was nursing him back to health.

"He kind of looks like a giant dog, doesn't he?"

Cassie raised an eyebrow. "Yeah...except for the part where he's a bear. And he's probably going to start tipping over our trash in search of some tasty morsels. You know what they say. It's best to let sleeping bears lie."

I wasn't sure that really *was* how the saying went. But I got her point.

"Okay," she said. "I'm ready to give you my not-so-expert opinion on Bud Blackburn's guilt or innocence."

When I finished filling her in on what I'd learned since she left for work this afternoon, she frowned. "Okay, let's work backward. Tanya's car goes over the cliff with this biker guy, Frank, behind the wheel and her in the trunk. If that was all we knew, the most obvious answer would be that Frank killed her and couldn't live with himself, but I'm pretty sure that's the wrong answer."

"I agree. It doesn't factor in Wren's brother getting beaten up, or why Bud, who clearly knew enough about everything to leave a trail of clues for me and for those snorkelers to find Tanya's car, didn't stop it. And while I didn't know this Frank, he doesn't strike me as the remorseful type. He'd have dumped her body in the river and taken the car. *And* it doesn't explain why her clothes were missing from her closet."

"Or why he put her in the trunk," Cassie said. "That's just weird. The second-most-likely scenario is that Bud did it. His mom found out, so he had to get rid of her."

I shrugged. "I really do think that was just an overdose. The question is whether she did it accidentally or intentionally. But I also think Blevins will try to pin everything on Bud, simply because it makes for a nice, tidy package with no loose ends."

She frowned. "Do you think there are any clues at Bud's house?"

"Maybe. But the only thing I'm likely to find is physical evidence that he painted those pictures, and I really don't have any doubt on that front. Getting in would probably be easy, since I suspect there's an excellent chance that the key is still hidden in a little slit on the underside of the doormat, just like it was back in 1987. But it probably has police tape across the door by now, and I have no doubt that Blevins would haul me in if I entered a crime scene. What I really need is to talk to Bud. He will talk to me, Cassie. And I'm pretty sure I know where he's hiding."

She thought for a long moment, and then said, "The place in the paintings, right? Torrance House? Do you think Blevins will check there?"

"Maybe," I admitted. "But Ed said it's poker night. Blevins, and most likely his deputies, will be occupied between nine and midnight."

"Is Ed going—"

"No. And neither are you. Neither is Wren. I have my phone. I have my pepper spray. And I have over a decade of experience as an investigative reporter. This is not a case where I need backup. I simply need to go and talk to him. Alone. He trusts me."

"I don't like this," Cassie said.

"I'm sure you don't," I told her, reaching over to squeeze her hand. "And you'll worry. Just like I did the first time you drove off in the car by yourself. Or when you took your first overnight trip with friends. Or spent the weekend with that guy you met in Memphis."

She laughed. "Okay. Your radar may have been right on that last one."

"But I didn't stomp my foot and say 'don't go!' did I? You're an adult. You have to make your own choices, even if they worry me sometimes. And this is my job."

"What did Ed have to say about this?"

"He's okay," I told her. "I bribed him with banana pudding."

She raised an eyebrow.

"Okay. I may also have subtly pointed out that his ex-wife being unwilling to accept the dangerous nature of his own job—a job that he was good at and that he loved—was what wrecked his marriage."

"You call that subtle?"

I laughed. "Maybe not. But he agreed. He said I should trust my instincts. And be careful. And I *will* be careful. I'll also call him if I feel that anything at all is off."

Even though I could tell from her expression that Cassie still wasn't happy with the situation, she said, "Okay.

I'm glad I have a good book to distract me." She stroked Cronkite, who was peacefully purring on the couch next to her. "How would you feel about taking a guard cat along?"

"Oh, that would work out wonderfully. You know full well I have to sedate him to even get him near the Jeep."

"We should get you a dog. A big one. You could name him Backup, like on *Veronica Mars*."

"Because Cronkite would happily share his living space with a big dog."

"Okay, then maybe you can just buy a leash for Remy."

I grinned. "Now *that* would be some very impressive backup."

☆ Chapter Eighteen ☆

A NEARLY FULL moon hung in the sky above my Jeep, and the wind whipping through the cracked window was warm and sweet. As I rounded the corner on River Road, I spotted the willow. There was a trace of blue reflecting back from its branches, but nothing like the almost-neon glow that had drawn my eye toward the tree in Bud Blackburn's painting. The tree still looked eerie and ominous, but that might have been because my imagination insisted on filling in the shadowy figures from the foreground of his other, less-finished work.

Beyond the tree, Torrance House was perched on a cliff like the remains of some giant beast. The driveway leading up to the hotel was little more than a gravel path after years of disuse, choked with weeds and tall grass that swayed in the breeze beneath the glare of my headlights. Torrance House looked forlorn and a little creepy.

That made me sad because I knew it in happier times. It had been a popular spot for weddings when I worked for Mr. Dealey, and I remembered people bringing in photographs from receptions, anniversary celebrations, and the like. The prom had apparently been held there until the gym was added to Thistlewood High in the late 1950s. It seemed a shame for a place that held so many good memories to be abandoned.

Although, possibly not *completely* abandoned at the moment. Once I cut the headlights, I detected a faint glow on one of the upper levels. It could have been reflected light or a light shining through from one of the houses on the far side of the river, but I didn't think so. I coasted forward at a few miles an hour, without headlights, thankful for the moonlight and hoping that any creatures, large or small, would be frightened away by the sound of the engine, since I'd have a hard time seeing them.

Before I left the house, I'd tried texting and then dialing the number that Bud had called me from this morning, even though I knew it was likely that Blevins would eventually get those phone records and ask why I'd called. Since no one had *officially* told me that Bud was on the lam, however, I had an excuse. I left a message saying that I was worried about how he was coping. That I hoped he was fine. That he should call if he needed to talk. All typical things that you might say to a grieving friend.

And Bud clearly did still consider me a friend, even though we'd had no contact in three decades. There had been no other person he'd thought to call when he found his mother's body on the floor that morning. Just me. That was sad, but I thought it might also be my one advantage. If Blevins reached Bud first, I suspected there would be a confession, real or coerced. And if Bud had anything to do with the killings, I thought the chances of a happy ending for him were pretty slim. Blevins would be more interested in a closed case that looked good come election time than he would be about justice for Bud Blackburn.

What scared me was that Bud seemed to have a pretty good sense of the gravity of his situation. I was more than a little worried that these paintings, vague though they may have been, were intended not merely as a confession, but as a *final* confession. While I was almost certain that Bud was at Torrance House, I was far less certain that I'd find him alive.

I pulled to a stop in front of the porch and shut the engine off. It was an almost perfectly silent night. I didn't even hear owls or crickets or any of the normal night sounds I'd grown accustomed to since moving back to Thistlewood. The only sound, and it was a faint one, was the murmur of the river beyond the building up ahead.

Bud's truck was nowhere in sight, but it could easily be parked on the other side of the building or in a garage. If he'd parked out in the open, I thought there was a decent chance that Blevins or one of his deputies would have spotted the truck and investigated. Bud might have realized that, too.

I stashed my pepper spray and phone in the pocket of my cardigan and got out of the Jeep, feeling vulnerable and exposed. Even though I really didn't think Bud would hurt me, I was on edge. In some ways, my feelings about Bud were very similar to my feelings about Remy. The bear might not *want* to hurt me, but I wasn't entirely sure how much control he had. It seemed that something had snapped inside Bud Blackburn, and it was that unpredictability that had me nervous.

Instead of heading straight inside, I walked around to the back of the house to check for signs of life. Crouching low, I peered around the corner. Beneath the large deck, I made out the headlights of what I was pretty sure was Bud's truck. The space was so narrow that I was amazed he'd managed to get the truck in there without taking out any of the support beams along the way.

I took a few steps toward the fence and looked down at the river. It was a good thing they'd built a barrier there. Aside from a few outcroppings of rock, it was almost a sheer drop to the river below.

My eyes traveled up the side of the building. A pale light flickered like a ghost behind one of the windows on the ground floor. For some reason, that faint, wavering light terrified me. My bravado about doing this on my own, without backup, sailed away on the night breeze. A wise person, someone with a sensible head on her shoulders, would get back in the Jeep and let the police handle this.

But apparently I was not that person. And while I definitely did not have a death wish, the guy inside that house was Tanya's brother. I took a deep breath and reminded myself that if Tanya had been here, she would have done whatever she could to help him. Odds were good that she'd have chewed him out royally after doing so, but Tanya would never have abandoned him to the questionable ethics of Steve Blevins.

The niggling, traitorous thought that Bud could well be the *reason* that Tanya isn't here crept back to the front of my brain, but I pushed it away. I didn't believe that. And because I didn't believe that, because I had a duty to Tanya, I would take some deep, calming breaths and then go back around to the front and simply knock. I would call out Bud's name, to be sure that he knew it was me and not Blevins. Just in case he had a gun.

When I reached the front of the house, however, Bud was standing between me and the Jeep. My heart began to pound so hard that my vision pulsed with it. One second Bud was in sharp focus, and the next he was a blur against the night sky.

"Hi, Bud," I said in a voice that sounded a bit like Minnie Mouse.

"Hey, Ruth," he said quietly. "I thought you might find me. You always were smart. I kind of wish you'd waited, though. Then you'd have just found the painting, not me, and this would have been easier."

Unsure exactly what he meant by that comment, I took a step away from him. He gave a frustrated laugh. "That came out all wrong. I'm not going to hurt you. I do have something I want to show you, though. I'd bring it out here if I could, but...I didn't have a canvas for this one. I had to use the wall."

He motioned toward the front entrance. "The door is open now. I had to go in through a window this afternoon, but I unlocked the door from inside so you wouldn't have to do that. But like I said, I really thought it would be *after*."

"After?"

He nodded. "After I was gone."

I hesitated, wanting to ask where he was going. But there was a note of finality to the word *gone* that left me little doubt as to what he meant. And so I followed him onto the porch, keeping one hand in the pocket of my cardigan, which held my phone and my tiny canister of pepper spray.

"This all happened a lot faster than I thought it would. I'm not really good at planning, and Mom...well, I didn't expect her to take all those pills. I guess she didn't want to be embarrassed when everyone found out. Or maybe arrested. I don't know. Can you be arrested for knowing a secret?"

"Depends on the secret. If it's about Tanya's death,

then maybe. The statute of limitations is probably up on anything other than murder, though."

He nodded. "Maybe it's better this way. If you see it before I'm gone. So I can answer any questions. Make sure you've got the story straight. Otherwise, what's the point of all this?"

That was a really good question, I thought. What *was* the point of all this?

"So, are you coming?" he asked.

"Sure," I said, mentally kicking myself and thinking that this was quite likely a horrible mistake. But I wanted to know. In for a penny, in for a pound.

Bud twisted the knob, and the door creaked open, exactly as you'd expect from the door to an abandoned hotel. The interior was dark, lit only by a flashlight Bud had propped up just inside the doorway and by a fainter light coming from the large open room up ahead. It looked like the glow of a candle, and I thought maybe it was the light I'd seen from below the deck.

"Your paintings are really good," I told him. "I think you could actually sell them."

"Really?" he said, clearly flattered. "My mom taught me to paint. She used to paint birds and flowers and stuff."

That surprised me. I'd never really thought of Sally Blackburn as creative. Or as someone who might have taken the time to pass that along to her son.

"She stopped after Tanya died," Bud said. "I did too,

for a while, but I couldn't *stay* stopped, you know? I like to paint."

"I can tell. But...why did you want me to think your paintings were by Ms. McBride?"

"So you'd want to see them. She was your favorite teacher, right?"

"Yes. But you could have sent them to the newspaper office. Or...you could have just come to talk to me about all of this."

"No," he said. "I couldn't. And like I said, it wasn't supposed to happen this fast. Everything moved *too fast*. I saw you going to Lucy McBride's house, and I thought that was my best chance, but I should have waited until after they found the car. I didn't think they'd find it so quick. I thought I'd have time to finish everything and be gone already."

We went through the doorway into an open room with a high ceiling and a large fireplace at one end. The smell of fresh paint hung in the air. So did the smell of bourbon. Some of that was coming from Bud, but also from the mostly empty bottle next to his paints.

"That's the last picture," Bud said, pointing to the wall. "I mailed you some papers, too. So you'd have them. Tanya's song notebook and some stuff I wrote down about all of this. Just in case you didn't figure it out from the paintings. This one would be a lot better if you'd found it during the day, though. I didn't count on you coming out here in the middle of the night. Why did you *do* that?"

Excellent question, I thought.

"Because the sheriff is looking for you," I told him. "I wanted to hear your story before he found you. Also, I wanted to tell you not to talk to him without a lawyer."

"You don't trust him, do you?"

"Not really." I squinted, wishing the light was better, and then remembered the flashlight app on my phone. It didn't help much.

This new picture took up most of the wall, but it almost looked as though the plaster had just been painted a different color. It was completely blue, with slight variations in tone. It seemed to be moving slightly, but that was probably the flickering light of the candle in the center of the room.

"I don't get it," I told him after staring at the painting for several seconds.

"Take a few steps back," he said calmly, almost like a teacher. "You're too close to see it."

So I did as he asked, again wishing that there was a stronger light in the room.

"How does it look now?"

I tilted my head, unsure of what he wanted me to say. It really didn't look any different to me. And then, slowly, it did.

The painting was still entirely blue. But now I could see depth. Layers. Rocks and other objects hiding below the surface.

"It's the river," I said.

He nodded, smiling. "Very good. That's exactly what it is."

"This is supposed to show where Tanya was."

"Yes. And where I'll be."

A chill washed over me, even though I'd been worried about exactly this. "What do you mean?"

"That's where I'm going. It's where I've always been going, and it just took me a really long time to see that. The night Tanya died is when it all ended for me, too. I tried to move on, but I couldn't just push it down like my parents did. A few months ago, I went out to Lover's Leap, to the spot where her car went over. I was going to jump then, but I realized that if I did that, Tanya might be stuck in that trunk forever. That seemed wrong. I needed to make sure someone found her. And now that they have...it's time to finish it."

"I can't let you do that, Bud."

He gave me a sad smile. "You can't stop me."

And I realized he was right. I really *couldn't* stop him. He outweighed me by at least sixty pounds. I was in better shape. I might even be able to outrun him. But I would be physically unable to keep him from walking onto that deck and swan-diving down to the river below.

What I could do, however, was hit the panic button on my phone. Ed was going to be scared, and I hated that. I also hated the fact that I'd made this big stand with him and with Cassie, and hours later, I was having to call in the cavalry.

But I didn't think Bud was bluffing. So my choices

were to make the call or risk his life. And no matter what he'd done in the past, I wasn't willing to do that.

Five finger taps on the power button, and the app would send a call to Ed. Assuming I had a signal out here. In retrospect, that wasn't a given, and that could be a huge flaw in my plan.

But I had to try.

One. Two. Three. Four. Five.

☆ Chapter Nineteen ☆

I WISHED there was some way I could check the phone without Bud knowing. Check to see if I'd even had a signal when I sent the SOS. Or better yet, send a message to let Ed know that it was Bud who was in danger, not me.

But that wasn't an option, so I'd just have to play for time and hope for the best.

"I know you're depressed, Bud. Between your mom and Tanya, it's not surprising. But you've still got your dad—"

"First off, my dad has cancer. He's got maybe a month or two. And second, my *dad* was the problem! Mom, too. If they'd let me tell the police what happened, maybe I'd have wound up in jail. Maybe they were right about that. But it wouldn't have been forever."

"It's awful that they wouldn't let you tell the police.

But maybe you could talk to a counselor now. To help you work through things."

"No." His eyes widened. "Dad said I couldn't. Not ever. And he was right. We'd have all gone to prison. That doesn't mean I killed Tanya, though. I know that's what you probably think, but I didn't."

"I never believed you killed her, Bud. If I had to guess, I'd say it was Frank Daniels. My only question is whether you were one of the guys who attacked Wren's brother."

There was a long pause. He stared at me, almost angrily. "You weren't supposed to figure that out yet. The thing with James, that was Frank's idea. He had a lot of bad ideas. At first I thought he was cool, you know? When I was a little kid, we'd all line up to watch the River Rats come roaring through town on holiday weekends. I always said I was going to ride with them. Saved up for my motorcycle—"

"I remember," I told him. "You mowed a lot of lawns."

He smiled, but then it faded. "Frank said he could get me in when I turned eighteen. And I could just ride with them until then. They were okay guys. Got into some fights, and maybe did some drugs, but nothing major. Frank had a thing for Tanya, though. He used to chat her up at the diner. Ask her to sing for him, because he'd heard her at one of the talent shows the year before. Find little excuses to touch or rub up against her. She thought he was a creep, and she was right." He shook his head. "I should've just killed him then and saved us all a lot of heartbreak later. Anyway, we were at the diner that day, on the Fourth, and Frank saw James come in. Said he was flirting with Tanya at the register. Called him some awful names when Tanya came over to refill our drinks. And she—"

"Cooled him off," I said. "Dumped the pitcher in his lap."

Bud nodded. "That was a mistake. Frank stormed outside, and when I went out to talk to him, he said he was going to make Tanya regret it. I got mad. Told him that was my sister he was threatening. Figured I'd end up having to fight him and that would not have ended well, I tell you. He would have mopped the pavement with me. But then he backed off."

"So what happened?"

Bud shrugged. "I'd signed on to work the shift up here, for that cocktail party, but I was supposed to meet up with Frank after. I didn't know James was working here, too. Frank pulled into the parking lot when James and a few of us were out back, finishing off some of the bottles before we tossed them into the dumpster. Then I saw Frank's taillights. I didn't stay for the cleanup detail. Rode back into town and met Frank down near the park. He said he had a chore to handle. Did I want to come or was I a sissy?"

He was quiet for several minutes. "I didn't know what he was planning, but I had a bad feeling when we headed back out this way. Kept hoping James had gotten a ride, or maybe Wren had come to pick him up. Or maybe whatever chore Frank was talking about was down at the marina or his grandma's campground. I followed on my bike, barely keeping up because his Harley was way faster, and he wasn't paying attention to the speed limit. He drove past the Torrance House driveway, and I was so relieved, but then he parked just inside the woods, past the willow and the clearing. Said we were just going to scare James a little. And I believed him. I shouldn't have. But I did."

Bud rubbed his face with his left hand. "Frank beat the crap out of James, right there on the side of the road." He shook his head sadly. "I didn't help. Even told him to stop, but I could have done more. I was scared. Scared I'd be next. He would've killed James, I think, but suddenly there were headlights on us. Frank had left a note on Tanya's car at the diner, telling her where she could pick her boyfriend up. She came storming out and shoved him away. I wish to God she *hadn't* come, and I know that's awful. James would have been dead, probably. But *she* wouldn't have been."

"Tanya stopped him?"

"Yeah. She yanked on his shirt collar, pulling him back. Frank swung his elbow back and she fell. Whacked her head against that weird fin by the headlights on the Mercury. She never got back up."

Tears were streaming down his face. Mine, too. I could envision Tanya, backlit by the headlights like an avenging angel. Which is exactly what she *had* been for James.

"She didn't get up," Bud repeated. "And I lost it. I pulled out my pocket knife and dove for Frank. He didn't even see it coming. I killed him right there by that willow tree. Tanya...she was already dead. I didn't know what to do. I dragged Frank and Tanya into the woods where we'd parked the motorcycles. James was alive, though. I put him in the car. Drove him to his grandma's house. Left him on the porch and rang the bell. Then I got out of there. Drove home. I didn't know what else to do."

He was quiet for a long time, and then he said, "I thought they'd call the police. But Dad drove back out with me. I didn't mention James. Figured I'd cross that bridge when we came to it. But it was probably a really good thing that I took James home. I don't know what my dad would have done if James had still been there. I think there's a good chance there would have been three bodies in that car."

Bud started crying again. Without even thinking, I reached out and touched his arm. He hardly seemed to notice.

"All I wanted to do was call the police and tell them everything. Dad wouldn't hear of it. He said there was nothing we could do for Tanya, and he wasn't going to lose everything he'd worked for over some good-for-nothing biker. He made me wait there while he drove back into town to get Tanya's things. And then we took the car up to Lover's Leap. Put Frank behind the wheel. Dad put Tanya in the trunk with her stuff. That was the only time I saw any emotion on his face that whole night."

I gave his arm a squeeze. "And then the two of you pushed the car over the edge?"

Bud nodded. "He said we'd tell everyone Tanya had just run away. Told me and Mom that we were never to speak of that night again. Never. I kept thinking the police would be knocking on my door anyway, because James would tell them about the fight. And I kind of wanted that to happen, because maybe he'd remember Tanya being there, too, and then I could tell them everything. I wanted to tell James I was sorry for being a coward. Try to make it up, you know? But he moved off to Chattanooga. I guess they never even called the police, because we'd have heard around town. There would have been talk."

I nodded. "They didn't call. He didn't remember much. I don't know if he even remembered Frank's name until we were talking about it today."

"You want to know the weird part, Ruth? I think my dad started to believe the story they made up. Mom, too. That's how they moved on. That's how they dealt with it." He shook his head and swallowed hard. "But I never could. And I don't want to try anymore."

With that, he sighed heavily and went to the door that led to the deck.

I ran after him. The weight of the phone in my pocket was maddening, jostling against my leg as I ran.

How long had it been since I sent the SOS? Had Ed even gotten my message?

Grabbing Bud's arm, I spun him around. "Stop it! You do *not* get to take the easy way out, Bud Blackburn!"

He looked at me in surprise. "What?"

"You heard me! You don't get to take the easy way out. Maybe your mom and dad didn't give you any choices back then, but you have them now. If you really mean it, if you really wanted to tell the truth back then, what's stopping you now?"

I was mostly playing for time. But I was also telling him *exactly* what his older sister would have said. "If you wanted to apologize to James, to try and make it right, what's stopping you now? You were sixteen back then. Tanya wouldn't blame you for what happened that night."

To be fair, I wasn't sure about that. I thought Tanya probably *would* have blamed him for what happened to James. But she wouldn't have wanted him to die for it.

Bud yanked away from me, and I knew in that instant that he'd been right earlier. If he decided to jump, there was no way I could stop him.

"No!" he bellowed. "I'm tired—"

"I don't care! And neither would Tanya. She would tell you to use the rest of your life making things right. To be a better person. Make a *difference*. If you jump, you're every bit the coward that you were that night. You owe it to your sister to make this right."

He reached out, and for a moment, I was certain that

Bud Blackburn was going to toss *me* over the edge of the deck. But then his arms went around me. All of the fight left his body. His shoulders began to shake. He dropped to his knees on the deck and cried.

I reached into my pocket and checked the phone. It had zero bars.

The cavalry was not on its way. And in the end, maybe that was for the best.

☆ Chapter Twenty ☆

I COULDN'T BRING myself to simply deliver Bud into the sheriff's hands, so as soon we hit a pocket of cell coverage, I called Ed and asked him to see if he could get an attorney to meet us at my office. Given how long Ed had served as sheriff, I was hoping he'd know at least one lawyer who would be willing to drop everything at nearly eleven on a Sunday night.

Bud was silent on the drive into town, but as we pulled into the parking lot behind the office, he looked over and gave me a teary smile. "Thank you, Ruth. For a moment there on the deck, it was almost like Tanya was yelling at me."

I shrugged and returned his smile. "I heard her yell at you enough times back in the day. Guess that helped me do a decent imitation."

"Do you think I'll go to prison?" he asked.

"I don't know. There's no statute of limitations on

murder. You were sixteen, though. You'll have to ask your attorney, but I'm sure that's a mitigating factor."

"But Blevins thinks I killed my mom."

That's the one thing that worried me most in all of this, but I tried to put on a brave face. "You'll have a lot of people willing to testify on your behalf, Bud. And your friendly local newspaper will be doing its best to dig up any evidence that might help you."

He sighed. "Do you think they let you paint in prison?"

"I think they might," I told him. "But hopefully you'll be able to set up your canvas and paint in your own backyard."

Ed and Wren were waiting in the front office when we arrived, and Ed said that Cassie was on her way. I probably should have told him to hold off on calling them, because poor Bud didn't need an audience. But it was too late now.

Bud flinched when he saw Wren, and I pulled him aside before we joined them. "That's your first step, Bud. The first step toward making it right. How many times did you sit down in the basement with me and Wren and Tanya, watching movies? Eating popcorn? She's a good person. You know that. So is James. I can't make any promises, but I think they'll give you a chance to make this right if you have the courage to take the first step. You don't need to talk to her right this minute. You're still upset. But you *do* need to do it."

Truthfully, I didn't *want* Bud to talk to Wren right

now. Wren and James would have every right to feel angry about the role Bud had played in James's injuries. They didn't owe him forgiveness. But while I didn't know James well enough to be certain how he'd react, I did know Wren, and I felt sure she'd get there eventually.

Bud gave a meek wave to the others and then sat down in one of the desk chairs.

"Are you okay?" Ed asked me.

"Yep. You found an attorney?"

"I did. With any luck, D'Arcy Jones will beat Blevins here. I *might* have called her first."

"Thank you." I gave him a quick kiss. I hadn't quite decided when I was going to admit to him and Cassie that I'd hit the panic button. I was sure that I'd tell them *eventually*, but maybe it could wait a bit.

"You are very welcome. And in fact, I think that's her now."

A young woman in a suit was standing at the front door, looking a bit tousled, like maybe she'd already been in bed when Ed called. He went to answer the door, and I turned back to Bud, who wasn't alone anymore. Wren was next to him. It was clear from his expression that he was grieving, and that's kind of Wren's Bat Signal.

By the time we'd introduced Bud to his attorney, Cassie and Blevins had both arrived. Cassie wrapped me in a warm, tight hug, and then Blevins leveled an angry scowl at me. It deepened when he saw the attorney seated next to Bud.

"Jones and Townsend." He huffed. "Why am I not

surprised that the two most annoying women in Woodward County know each other?"

D'Arcy Jones and I exchanged a look. We hadn't
even been introduced yet. Ed had taken her straight over
to her new client. I was now quite certain, however, that
she was someone worth knowing. Anyone who annoyed
Blevins was a-okay in my book.

"So let me guess. Mr. Blackburn just strolled into
your office, in the middle of the night?" Blevins said.
"Where you and your attorney friend—along with Ed
and everyone else—just *happened* to be waiting?"

"Something like that," Ed told him.

"Bud didn't have anything to do with his mom's
overdose," I said. "But I think he can fill in some
gaps on what happened to his sister and Frank
Daniels thirty-two years ago. As long as you ask
those questions in the presence of his attorney, of
course."

Cassie, who was seated at the desk behind me, snick-
ered. That earned her a venomous look from Blevins, but
he didn't say anything. He just stalked over to Bud and
began reading him his rights.

I was at the door a few minutes later when Blevins
led him away. Bud looked nervous. I squeezed his arm
and whispered, "Tanya would be so proud of you, Bud.
So proud."

"Proud that he's being arrested," Blevins said. "Yeah,
right."

I barely resisted the urge to kick him in the shin.

The police car pulled away from curb, followed immediately by D'Arcy Jones in a little white Prius.

"I'm going to buy her lunch soon," I told Ed. "She seems nice."

"She's nice unless you mess with her clients," he said. "Then she turns into a tiger."

Wren looked out the window at the receding tail-lights. "I didn't quite follow everything he was saying about James. I gather it was this Frank guy—"

"Frank Daniels," I told her. "He's the one responsible for James's injuries. Bud was an onlooker. And Tanya... Well, Bud seemed to think that she was the only reason that James didn't die that night."

I spent the next few minutes bringing them up to speed on everything that Bud had told me.

"So Tanya's parents knew all along," Wren said. "They just lied to us."

"Basically. Bud said they coped by just burying it. Pretending it never happened, and that Tanya was still out there somewhere. But that didn't work for him. He couldn't cope with the guilt, both about Tanya and about what happened to James. I don't think he felt all that guilty about Frank, to be honest."

"Nor should he," Wren said, with more venom in her voice than I'd ever heard.

"So, how did you talk him down from the ledge?" Cassie asked.

"Very carefully. Mostly I just reminded him that Tanya had loved him. That she wouldn't want him to take the coward's way out. She'd want him to make it right. And I think he'll try his best to do that."

"I hope...so," Wren said. A huge yawn punctuated the sentence and quickly spread around to the rest of us.

Cassie laughed. "I think that's our cue to head home. Tomorrow may be Memorial Day, but we're hoping to open the new shop—which I think we're going to call The Buzz—by the first week of July. So between now and then, pretty much every day will be a workday for me and Dean." She didn't sound at all displeased about that. I was looking forward to sitting down with her, now that the craziness of the past few days was over, and hearing all about their plans.

"I thought I had the day off," Wren said. "But Bud just told me that they'll be holding the services for Sally Blackburn at Memory Grove, so I'm going to need to meet with her sister tomorrow."

"And Ed," I told them, "has a book to finish."

"Nope." He grinned widely. "I told you I was almost finished, didn't I? I'd just emailed the draft for *Blood and Ashes* about two minutes before you called. And yes, I forwarded you a copy. That means I actually get to take tomorrow off."

I gave him a fake pout. "I've been waiting months, and now I won't even have a chance to start reading it until Tuesday. The proof is due at the printer tomorrow, and I have to redo the entire front page now."

"So I guess we'd all better go home and get some sleep," Wren said.

"Sleep? Who has time for that? I just need one of you to bring me coffee."

★★★

NEXT UP: A sneak peek at A SEANCE IN FRANKLIN GOTHIC (Thistlewood Star Mysteries #3)

Sneak Peek: A Séance in Franklin Gothic
(Thistlewood Star Mysteries #3)

☆ Chapter One ☆

THE MAN SMILED as the woman leaned in, her eyes bright and shining. She knew exactly what she wanted, and he was more than happy to comply.

I leaned over the railing and positioned my Nikon to catch a few more shots. These were exactly what I needed for the front page of this week's *Thistlewood Star*.

He knew they needed to hurry, though, so he didn't waste time with chitchat. The man simply asked the woman's name and jotted a brief message across the blank page. Then he scrawled his signature below and smiled again before moving on to the next person in line.

It was a very impressive line, too, especially for a small town like Thistlewood, Tennessee. The Buzz, Thistlewood's newest business, had been open for three weeks, but this was the official grand opening. It was also the release party for Ed Shelton's latest mystery, *Even in Death*. Most of Thistlewood had turned out for the event, along with a smattering of tourists and people from neighboring towns. I recognized a lot of their faces, including a few that I'd pretty much guarantee hadn't read a book in years. Most of them knew Ed from his years as sheriff of Woodward County. That was before I moved back to Thistlewood, but by all accounts, he'd been a very good sheriff. When an accident had forced his retirement seven years ago, he'd simply shifted to solving fictional crimes instead.

I'd already gotten one of the shots that I'd use for my article—Ed leaning back against the brick wall, next to a table stacked with copies of his two books. He looked darn good for sixty-one, and I felt a warm flush of pride. He'd worked hard and deserved this more than anyone I knew. And, yes, I would have thought that even if he wasn't, as many of his fictional characters would no doubt put it, my main squeeze.

Wren Lawson, my best friend and proprietor of the local funeral home, joined me at the railing that looked down over the main floor of the bookstore. She was carrying a mug of something that smelled like coffee but was barely even beige. A milky white dot that almost looked like a flower decorated the center.

"What is this?" I asked as she handed me the cup.

"That is a white chocolate flat white. Your daughter

swears it's coffee. And she says she made it especially for you, so you have to drink it."

I glanced toward the counter near the center of the mezzanine where my daughter, Cassie, was serving coffee and slinging pastries like a pro. Dean Jacobs, the local mailman and the owner of the shop, was also behind the counter, but there was no question who was running things. He might be the boss on paper, but he was only around in the evenings and on weekends. He'd hired Cassie to take charge, and she had...with a vengeance.

"Oh, the perils of motherhood," I said before taking an experimental sip of the brew. "It's not bad. But it's also not coffee. More like coffee-scented hot chocolate."

"Dean was onto something with all this," Wren said, looking around. "Especially upstairs. I had no idea esports was even a thing."

"Neither did I." To be honest, I was amazed that the idea had worked. Not the bookstore, which Thistlewood had needed. The Buzz carried mostly used books, something that's always welcome in a tourist town. People have plenty to do when the sun is shining, with the Freedom River just a few miles away and a slew of tourist attractions within easy driving distance. Evenings and rainy days, however, generally found people crowding into the diner, just down the street, rather than being holed up in their rental cabins. Escaping into a book was a welcome relief from trying to put together a jigsaw puzzle that was missing five pieces or from listening to the kids whine about the cabin's lack of Wi-Fi and the cell coverage up here in the mountains, which is spotty at best and often downright abysmal.

The coffee shop was clearly needed, too. Pat's Diner was generally packed, and even the takeout line was intimidating in mid-summer. Once you got in, Patsy was quick to tell you that she only served real coffee, not the lattes, espressos, and cappuccino concoctions that so many vacationers seemed addicted to. And the one food truck in the park that had coffee on the menu served up a brew so strong that it could deadlift a horse.

But the idea of adding an esports area upstairs had been sheer genius. Dean had a contractor soundproof the upper floor and put in twenty top-of-the-line gaming computers. Parents were happy to cough up the cash for their kids—and often, for themselves—to spend a few hours playing their favorite multiplayer games online. And the non-gamers could hang out downstairs, drinking coffee and reading, while they waited.

In retrospect, Dean probably hadn't even needed the soundproofing he'd put in upstairs. On the few occasions I'd ventured up to eBuzz to check things out, the large room was nearly as quiet as the bookstore, with each of the gamers wearing headphones. Aside from an occasional whoop of victory, the loudest noise was the hum of the computers.

Wren finished the last of her own not-quite-coffee and said, "Tell Ed I said congratulations. I'll just get him to sign my copy next time I see him. I still need to bake some cookies and get some things together for the yard sale. You're still coming early to help me get things set up, right?"

"Absolutely. Can't wait."

Wren laughed. "Now you're just lying. But I do appreciate the help." She gave me a quick hug and began winding her way toward the door.

Crowds really aren't my thing, and now that Wren was gone, my inner introvert was pushing me to find a secluded corner where I could hide out. I'd already gotten all of the information and photos I needed for my story. Normally, I'd go hang with either Cassie or Ed, but they were both working. I scanned the room and noticed Ed's sister Sherry at a small table in the closest thing to a secluded corner I was likely to find.

As the youngest of the Shelton clan, Sherry had been a few years behind me in school, so I hadn't really known her all that well. Ed's other sister, Kim, had been closer to my age. She was living with her husband out in Texas, where they bought old homes, fixed them up, and flipped them. Made a pretty good living, too, from what I'd heard. Unlike Kim, Sherry had stayed in Thistlewood. She'd married a long-haul trucker, Jason Hanson, who had died of a heart attack a few months before I moved back to Thistlewood.

You'd never know Sherry had experienced a fairly recent loss to look at her. There was always a smile on her cheerful, round face. She'd simply thrown herself into her work—she ran an online tourism agency—and focused on their daughter, Kate, who had just started her senior year at Thistlewood High.

Sherry looked up and waved as I approached the table. "Ruth! Will you just look at Ed? I'm so proud of him."

"So am I." I motioned to the empty chair across from her. "Mind if I join you?"

"Of course. You don't even have to ask. You know that."

I pulled the chair out and sat down. "Where's Ms. Kate tonight?"

"Out with friends." Sherry rolled her eyes. "I told her she should come out and support her uncle, but looking at the crowd, I guess that wasn't really necessary, was it? And she had an activity with this Thistlewood Hands club. They always seem to be doing something."

"Thistlewood Hands? Did they even have that when we were in school?"

She shook her head. "It's fairly new, I guess. A service club. They clean up the highways and the park. Hold fundraisers. That sort of stuff."

"How's she doing?" I asked. "I haven't seen either of you in ages."

"Oh, we're both doing fine. Kate's diving straight into her senior year, although it really doesn't seem like they should start school at the end of July like they do. Back in the day, we used to get the whole summer. Anyway, she's getting ready to apply to the University of Tennessee. Hard to believe she's almost grown."

"I'm glad to hear she's planning to stay close to home," I said. "Has she decided on a major?"

Sherry laughed. "Yes. Four or five different majors, and that was just over the summer. But I guess most people change their majors at least a few times after they start college."

"True. Not me, though. I knew I was going to be a journalist after my first week working at the *Star*."

"Mr. Dealey was so proud of you, too. A friend of mine worked with him during our senior year and she said he bragged all the time about how you went on to work at the biggest paper in the state."

"And here I am, right back where I started," I said, laughing.

Prior to my move back to Thistlewood, I'd spent nearly twenty-five years, first as a reporter and then as an editor, with the *Nashville News-Journal*. When they were bought out by one of those large national newspaper chains and began downsizing, they'd offered me an early retirement package. After some hesitation, I'd decided to take it. That was about the same time that my husband, the man I'd been with even longer than I had with the *News-Journal*, decided he also wanted to downsize. When I'd left for college at age seventeen, I would have sworn on a stack of Bibles that I would never, ever move back to this tiny town. But I'd never sold the house just outside of town that my parents left to me. My best friend, Wren, had already moved back to Thistlewood to run the funeral home. And five years after Jim Dealey's death, the *Thistlewood Star* had still been looking for a new owner.

It was almost as if someone had painted a giant arrow in the sky pointing toward Thistlewood. This Way to Ruth Townsend's Second Act.

And so, I'd piled my things into the Jeep and headed back to the mountains. The only thing I'd really missed in Nashville, aside from decent cell phone coverage, was my daughter. A few months later, Cassie had decided to make the move as well.

Sherry was looking over at the table where Ed was chatting with readers. "In some ways, I think Ed was destined for this. He loved law enforcement, and he was a really good sheriff. Unlike that snake Blevins who replaced him. But Ed has always been a storyteller. When I was a little girl, I looked forward to the nights when he was home. Whatever book Mama or Daddy was reading to me, it didn't matter. It got pushed aside. I liked the stories Ed made up for me so much better."

I motioned toward the long line of people waiting to have their book signed and smiled. "Looks like you're not the only one who likes his stories."

She nodded, and then leaned forward, whispering across the table like she was sharing some deep secret. "I have to be honest, though. Ed really does have a gift for words, but his imagination can be a little dark sometimes. I prefer the stories he told me as a little girl. They usually had a princess and a dragon. Maybe even a unicorn. He'd always make them a little bit scary, but not so much that

I'd have nightmares. His last book was too intense for me. So much death and murder. There's enough of that in real life. I'd really rather read a nice romance, wouldn't you?"

"Oh, I don't know. A little romance in the mix is fine. But mysteries have always been more my thing."

"And that's why the two of you are perfect for each other." Sherry's eyes traveled behind me to the front door. "Speaking of mysteries, that woman looks like one of those femme fatales from Ed's books, doesn't she? All she needs is a trench coat and a pistol."

I turned to look and saw a tall young woman with hair the color of a copper penny in the doorway. She was beautiful, as pale and thin as a runway model. The door closed behind her with a little hiss, blowing her long tresses aside to expose a long, graceful neck.

"She's definitely not from here," Sherry said.

I managed to fight back a chuckle, which was good since I'd probably have had to explain it. Wren and I often laughed about the Thistlewood hierarchy. There was *from-here*, which— depending entirely on who was doing the assessment—could mean anything from starting kindergarten in Thistlewood to having a pedigree that went back three generations. Everyone else was *not-from-here*. Wren and I had both fallen into that latter category, since we didn't arrive in Thistlewood until our early teens. We'd both had a bit of a tough time due to our *not-from-here* status until Tanya Blackburn, who was sort of the queen bee of our class, took us under her wing.

Wren's situation had been worse than mine, truthfully, since Woodward County is about as *un*diverse as you can get.

Sherry's eyes widened. "Ruth. She's coming this way."

I turned sideways in my chair just as the young woman came to a stop next to our table. She didn't look at me, not at first, anyway. Her bright green eyes were locked on Sherry.

"Are you Sherry Hanson?"

Sherry nodded, giving the newcomer a confused smile. "Yes. I'm sorry. Have we met?"

"Actually, we haven't met. I'm Mindy Tucker. Your niece."

"My niece?" Sherry said with a nervous little laugh. "I'm sorry. There must be some mistake."

The girl sighed. "I hate springing this on you so suddenly, but I thought it might be best to talk to you first. I'm afraid this will be a bit of a shock for your brother, and...I thought it might help if there was someone else with him when he and I speak for the first time. I considered sending a message, but...some things really do need to be handled in person, don't you think?"

"Wait a minute," I said. "Are you saying you're Ed's... daughter?" Even as my mind dismissed the words, my eyes searched her face for any resemblance to Ed. I couldn't see any. Of course, that didn't mean it wasn't true.

Sherry looked a bit like she'd swallowed a lemon.

Was she angry or embarrassed? "Ed doesn't have a daughter."

The smile vanished from Mindy's face. "Apparently, that's not true. My mother didn't tell me until recently. I haven't been able to screw up the courage to contact him, but we're in town for a gig and I was walking by and I saw the poster."

A gig? Did she mean a temp job? That made no sense. Much of Thistlewood's economy is seasonal, dependent on tourism, and the current drought had cut deeply into the number of visitors. Businesses were laying people off early, not hiring new temps.

"It was sort of like...fate," the girl continued. "Like this was meant to be our first meeting."

I opened my mouth to point out that the launch party for Ed's book would, in fact, be a very bad time for their first meeting. But I never got the words out. The front door banged open. All three of us jumped and turned toward the entrance.

Ed's niece stood framed in the doorway. Her long blonde hair was a tangled mess, plastered to her face by sweat.

"Kate?" Sherry leaned forward. "Are you okay?"

The girl looked around wildly, clutching the doorway to keep her balance. Sherry stood up so quickly that her chair toppled to the ground, and she ran toward her daughter. I glanced over at the signing table and saw Ed excusing himself to the people in line as he pushed himself to his feet.

Sherry reached Kate within seconds, pulling her away from the open door and guiding her toward a chair. Kate moved like she was on autopilot, her eyes wide and vacant.

"Katie," Sherry said, kneeling down next to the girl. "What's wrong, honey? Talk to me."

Kate blinked and looked around. She seemed a little startled, almost as if she was seeing her surroundings for the first time. Then she said something in a jagged whisper that I couldn't make out, aside from the single word: Tessa.

Sherry couldn't decipher it either. "What is it, baby? I can't understand you. You're scaring me."

Ed touched my shoulder. "What happened?"

"Something with Tessa Martin," Sherry said in a low voice.

Hearing Tessa's name seemed to have cut through Kate's fog. She looked up at Ed, and then back at her mom. "Tessa's dead," she said, choking back a sob. "She called it. Tessa called it, and it came and got her."

✪ Order A SÉANCE IN FRANKLIN GOTHIC ✪

About the Author

 C. Rysa Walker is the pen name author Rysa Walker adopts when she's in the mood to tackle mysteries that are a little more grounded in reality than her various science fiction and fantasy series. Occasionally, author Caleb Amsel is her partner in crime on these adventures. Learn more about the Thistlewood Star series on Rysa's website.

www.rysa.com/mysteries

Copyright © 2019 C. Rysa Walker

All rights reserved.

Originally published as Jessa R. Archer

No part of this book may be reproduced in any form or by any electronic or mechanical means, including information storage and retrieval systems, without written permission from the author, except for the use of brief quotations in a book review.

Publisher's Note: This is a work of fiction. Names, characters, places, and incidents are a product of the author's imagination. Locales and public names are sometimes used for atmospheric purposes. Any resemblance to actual people, living or dead, or to businesses, companies, events, institutions, or locales is completely coincidental.

Cover Design: Rysa Enterprises, Inc.

Palatino for the Painter/C. Rysa Walker. — 1st ed.

Made in the USA
Monee, IL
18 March 2023

30115704R00135